PRAISE FOR THE INSPECTOR DAVID
GRAHAM MYSTERY SERIES

"I'm in love with him and his colleagues."
"A terrific mystery."
"These books certainly have the potential to become a PBS
series with the likeable character of Inspector Graham and
his fellow officers."
"Delightful writing that keeps moving, never a dull
moment."
"I know I have a winner of a book when I toss and turn at
night worrying about how the characters are doing."
"Totally great read!!!"
"Refreshingly unique and so well written."
"Alison outdid herself in this wonderfully engaging
mystery, with no graphic violence or sex."
"This series just gets better and better."
"DI Graham is wonderful and his old school way of doing
things, charming."
"Great character development."
"Kept me entertained all day."
"Wow! The newest Inspector Graham book is outstanding."
"Great characters and fast paced."

THE CASE OF THE PRETTY LADY

ALSO BY ALISON GOLDEN

THE CASE OF THE PRETTY LADY

ALISON GOLDEN

GRACE DAGNALL

Cover Illustration: Richard Eijkenbroek

Published by Mesa Verde Publishing
P.O. Box 1002
San Carlos, CA 94070

ISBN-13: 978-0-9887955-2-5

Edited by
Marjorie Kramer

"Reading is to the mind what exercise is to the body."
~*Joseph Addison*

To get your free copy of *The Case of the Screaming Beauty,* the prequel to the Inspector David Graham series, plus two more books, updates about new releases, exclusive promotions, and other insider information, sign up for Alison's mailing list at:

https://www.alisongolden.com/graham

CHAPTER ONE

EVEN BEFORE THEY heard him speak, his bulk, the brilliantly white Stetson, and his endearing manner marked him as an American tourist. "You know what I'm wondering?" the man boomed in a Texan drawl. "I'm wondering what on the good Lord's earth a *fo'c'sle* is." He pronounced it "fock-slee," to the amusement of the early lunchtime crowd. "Anyone want to educate a newcomer?" he asked the two-thirds empty bar.

The barman, Lewis Hurd had this covered and not for the first time. "A 'forecastle'," he explained. "It's the front part of the deck of a working ship or a warship."

"You don't say," the American replied. "And how the heck do you pronounce it?"

The regulars at the bar replied in an oft-rehearsed chorus, "Fock-sul."

"Awesome," the American beamed. "But what's a *ferret* doing on a *warship?*"

Hurd leaned in to handle this one while the pub's patrons, here for the dependable grub or to enjoy the handcrafted ales alongside like-minded souls, returned to their conversations.

Over in the corner, an invective of French rose into the air, followed by a roar of approval. Five men in boots and work pants stood talking over one another as they drank their pints. One man poked a finger at another who gesticulated rapidly as he defended himself against some unknown accusation. The ferocity of their discussion would have seemed threatening were it not for the smiles on the faces of their countrymen. Soon words gave way to back thumps and clinking glasses, gestures that told the other pub-goers that all was well.

Lewis Hurd looked at the group, barely concealed dislike curling his lip. "Keep your voices down, lads, please," he called over, his words more reasonable than the feelings his expression conveyed.

Beyond them, by the big, paned windows with their view of the harbor, Tamsin Porter and Greg Somerville, two thirty-somethings, fit and trim in their high-end outdoor wear, were sitting in sullen silence, refusing to even look at one another. Tamsin stared into her half-finished pint, her hands fiddling with the cord that circled the perimeter of her jacket's hood while Greg let his gaze wander over the masts of the boats in the harbor and the members of a crew who chatted as they sheltered from a sudden downpour beneath a barely sufficient awning.

"So, you're not going to say anything?" Tamsin asked, finally.

Greg sighed, the momentary peace brought to an unwelcome end. "What do you want me to say, Tamsin?"

"I don't know. Something. Anything."

"Shall I stand up, right here," he proposed, "and admit

to the whole pub that I'm a poor scientist? Would that do you?"

"Greg, come on..."

"Or that I'm an unreliable partner, that I can't source enough funding for more robust trackers, and therefore my data can't be trusted?" His temper rose quickly, along with his voice. "That I should have found a way to become clairvoyant and *predicted* that our work might be interrupted by a freak storm?"

Tamsin pushed her pint away and folded her arms. "Calm down, all right?"

"I can't stand to hear you complain about my anger when you're the one who does the most to create it. Why don't you stop criticizing and *help* for once?"

Their relationship, once admired by their friends for its stability and endurance, was in a strange, disappointing, some might say vicious spiral. They didn't talk any more. They just argued and nit-picked and called each other terrible names, only to apologize the next day, and begin the acrimony all over again, the day after that.

"We're going to get some good data," Greg promised. "They're coming in, maybe eight or ten of them, and if one comes anywhere near a buoy, we'll pick up the UHF signal, and we'll know *exactly* where our little beauties are traveling to."

"*If* the hurricane doesn't shift their behavior patterns," Tamsin countered.

The rotund American was still wandering around the pub, drink firmly in hand, examining the photos and old examples of fishing gear nailed to the walls. "Tell me, are you guys from out of town, too?" he asked them cheerily, oblivious to the tension simmering between the couple.

Tamsin made no move to even look up, but Greg was glad of the distraction. "We are, but we're working here," he said.

"On what?" the American asked.

Tamsin turned, her eyes tired and still a little swollen from crying earlier. She said simply, "Sharks."

The American's eyes widened, a reaction the couple was used to. "Get outta here," he breathed. "What do you do?"

"We're marine biologists. We're involved in a British government project to track the population of Holden Sharks. This is our third year tracking them."

"Huh!" It was that curious, open-minded sound that meant, "Say more about that."

"They migrate through the English Channel, but no one's proven where they go to breed. We're here to gather that data."

"Neat!" the American exclaimed. "I've never heard of a...what're they called, again?"

Greg folded his arms. "Holden sharks. They're among the rarest in the world," he explained. "Little bit like a basking shark," he added, pointing to a photo on the wall which showed the giant, unlikely animal approaching the camera, its jaw cranked open to reveal not teeth, but rows of fleshy filters, like those of a whale. "And they head through here on their way to the Norwegian Sea, where they mate, feed, and then head back toward the open Atlantic."

"At least," Tamsin interrupted, her fingertip pressing to the table in a sudden rush of frustration. "We *think* that's what they do. Opinions vary." She gave Greg a sideways glance, the now-obvious, strange, electric tension between the pair telling the American visitor that the theory was a major bone of contention between them. "We need the data from our buoys to support any conclusions. It may be that they simply turn around here for some reason and head straight back out."

Greg wouldn't let this go. "That's highly unlikely and you know it," he said, well aware that they were restarting a two-year-old argument in front of a bemused layman. "Sharks don't do one-eighties unless they're lost."

"What about those whale sharks in the Gulf of Thailand?" Tamsin argued. "They swam up there and turned right around."

The American nodded politely to them both and wandered off, unwilling to be neither enabling party, nor participant, in this increasingly bitter confrontation.

"Case in point," Greg retorted. "They were lost and corrected their path."

Before Tamsin could compose a counterpoint, the swing door next to them burst open and a man walked in, shaking himself dry. The moisture from his waterproofs caught the light in the dim, dingy bar as drips tracked his movements on the floor.

Surprised, Tamsin and Greg looked up, Greg immediately stiffening while Tamsin resumed fingering her hood's drawstring. When he caught sight of them, the man's eyes widened with shock, but he took a step toward them, his hand extended.

"Tamsin, Greg," he acknowledged, looking at them in turn.

"Kev, what're you doing here?" Greg ignored the outstretched hand, but Tamsin filled the uncomfortable void and shook it.

"Just came in out of the rain."

"Not here, *here*. On Jersey. You're not following us

again, are you? You know we have a permit, right? And government funding."

"Yeah, I heard." Kev sounded like he'd heard it more than once, too.

Greg half-rose from the bench he was sitting on, his anger along with the volume of his voice increasing again. "Listen, you have no right—"

"Greg..." Tamsin put a warning hand on his arm, and he wavered. He carefully sat down again, catching sight of Lewis Hurd carefully watching the trio as he slowly polished a glass behind the varnished, wooden bar top.

"Be on your way, Kev. We better not see you out on the water, okay?" she said.

"Nice to see you, too. " The man shrugged and sidled off, dragging from his head the woolen beanie that held his bushy hair in check and brushing drops from his beard.

"That's all we need. Another animal rights pain in the bum. If you want to complain about someone, Tamsin, complain about them. Why don't they do their homework and understand that what we do will sustain the herd, not threaten them?"

Greg stood suddenly, forcefully enough to jar the table. The warming remains of Tamsin's pint wobbled dangerously. She moved to steady it.

"The weather's fairing up," he told her, "and I'm due out to collect the in-situ data from the buoys. This might be the last time for a few days given the forecast. You can come with me, or sit here and continue telling the whole pub what a rubbish scientist I am." He grabbed his jacket. "It's entirely up to you." Greg stomped out of the bar and up the stairs to the room they'd been sharing above the pub, leaving Tamsin feeling hollow and strangely abandoned.

Lewis Hurd sidled over to collect Greg's empty mug

and returned to the bar silently. Tamsin continued to stare at her drink, but as she pushed it away again, she saw Greg leave the pub and watched him out of the window heading down to his small motor launch, wondering what had happened to the fun, loving relationship they'd once had. And also wondering just how long the strained, combative one that had replaced it could possibly last.

Greg could see the damage from a quarter mile away through his powerful binoculars. "Damn it," he cursed as he applied the left rudder, bringing his small boat gradually alongside the cracked, orange buoy. Sixteen of the buoys, arranged in a pattern between the Portland and Thames sea areas, were intended to give Greg and Tamsin the clearest picture yet of Holden shark movements in the Channel. But this one would never transmit again. The bright orange chassis had split, exposing the buoy's electronic innards to the raging sea. The wind was getting up, and Greg cursed again as he struggled to winch the buoy on board. "How did this happen?"

He sat down in the boat as he examined the buoy. He felt emotionally drained. The constant arguing with Tamsin was wearing on his nerves, and as he'd prepared to leave the harbor earlier, he'd been heckled by a couple of locals. The fishermen resented their presence every year, although there was no evidence to suggest that their methods for collecting data affected the fishermen or their catch at all. The sight of Kev Cummings in the pub had just added to his troubles. Kev was the regional director of the local SeaWatch chapter, a grand title for someone who was, in Greg's opinion, a simple yob. Their annual game of "cat and mouse" was a complication he found tiresome. It was exhausting to be the villain when all you were doing was your best to protect the marine ecosystem, ultimately for everyone's benefit. *If only they could see that.*

Greg frowned at the mess of salt-corroded wires, so bent and misshapen as to be almost unrecognizable. Two wires twisted impotently in the air. The ends were clean cut. Greg stood, feet apart, in the gently swaying boat, the buoy lying easily in his hands as he stared at the horizon. His eyes darkened as his fury built once more. The impending poor weather had driven seafarers ashore early and sidelined the commercial vessels transporting tourists seeking cheap booze from the coastal French hypermarkets. Greg looked around. With the exception of one boat some distance away, he was alone on the water.

He put the buoy aside and set course for the next one. In theory, each time a shark passed by the buoy's receptors, the tiny transponders within the shark's skin would activate, transmitting a long-term record of the animal's depth, speed, and course. Although sharks turned suddenly for all kinds of reasons, Greg's thesis was that they were migrating generally *east*, and that they ultimately emerged in the North Sea where they patrolled off the coast of Norway as they waited for potential mates to arrive. His data would settle long-standing questions about shark behavior and perhaps help to raise money and awareness for shark conservation. *Jaws* had done enduring harm to the reputation and safety of sharks all over the world, and Greg felt a moral duty to do his part in reversing some worrying trends.

Not everyone saw his research like that, however. Animal activists were a constant irritant to marine biologists. Some felt the moral imperative was to leave the sharks entirely alone, to allow them to continue their natural behavior, honed over centuries, unencumbered by man's efforts to understand them. Others believed that any study was bound to disrupt the animals, provide false data, and even threaten their existence.

Greg found the activists to be largely willful, illogical, and uneducated in the ways of the animals they claimed to be trying to protect. As far as he was concerned, they romanticized the sharks and imagined the threat posed by his research. Thankfully, they usually went no further than making their presence felt on land in low-key ways; they would hang around the launch site or "bump" into him and Tamsin around town. Neither of them felt particularly intimidated, nor did the activists seek to intervene directly in their work. This new possibility that his research was being actively sabotaged represented a significantly increased level of intimidation, one that was concerning, and most definitely dangerous to the sharks. Even perhaps himself.

His next buoy lay a mile away, Day-Glo orange and gratifyingly upright. Like an iceberg, the waves concealed much of its mass. Below the surface, a weighty ballast kept the buoy steady while the orange tower above helped fend off collisions in these busy sea lanes. Greg pulled alongside and reached over to open a panel and slot in a cable. He then waited the requisite ten seconds with his fingers crossed, and checked his phone for the data flow. "Green across the board. Sweet."

Only after he'd returned to the boat's modest pilot house and given the data a cursory examination did he see the good news: *six* Holden sharks had come through over the past three days. Forgetting his earlier concerns, he slapped the boat's wheel and hooted. "Yes!"

Preoccupied with jubilation, he sensed nothing untoward until there was an unexpected noise behind him, sudden and firm, as though something large had collided hard with the stern of his boat. Greg was thrown forward hard onto his hands and knees and shook his head roughly as the sound of feet landing on the deck of his motor launch reached his ears.

CHAPTER TWO

D ETECTIVE INSPECTOR DAVID Graham
cleared his throat and tapped gingerly on the side
of a glass with the end of his fountain pen.
"Fellow officers," he began, his glass raised to the man of the
hour, "I give you Constable Barry Barnwell, now *twice*
presented with the Queen's Gallantry Medal by Her
Majesty at Buckingham Palace!" He broke into applause,
accompanied by Sergeants Janice Harding and Jim Roach.
The four of them were in his office. "It is an honor to serve
the community alongside an officer of your caliber,
Constable Barnwell."

Blushing, but feeling as proud as he'd been since those
two remarkable occasions in London, Barnwell shook his
boss's hand and took a polite sip of his lemonade.

"Congratulations again, mate," Jim said next, as Janice
found some jazz music on an Internet radio station. Graham
closed the office door almost completely, but not quite. The
day's investigations were formally over, but they still had to
respond to any members of the public who walked or
rang in.

Barnwell smiled to himself and focused on enjoying the moment, glowing with satisfaction. If he were honest, or if Harding prodded him long enough, he'd admit this little gathering meant just as much as a visit to the Palace.

"I mean it," Graham told him as they stood together. "You could have had your pick of assignments after the first QGM, but now... Any thoughts on what you might do?"

Barnwell looked surprised for half a second. "My only plan is to continue on here, sir." He blinked a couple of times, and then added, "That is, of course, if it's all right with you?"

It was Graham's turn to be surprised. "All right?" he repeated. "You're a remarkable officer. I'd like ten more of you." Graham raised his glass again, "To Gorey Constabulary and its officers. A small, but highly effective unit comprised of some of the best officers I've ever had the pleasure to work with."

"Very kind, sir," Janice replied.

"Not at all, Sergeant. It's well-deserved." Graham wandered over to pour himself another drink.

"I couldn't help noticing," Roach said leaning in to Janice, "that you're glancing at your watch a lot. Are we keeping you from something?"

"Nothing escapes your perceptive faculties does it, Roachie?" Harding smirked. "It's Jack. He should be here soon."

"How are things going with him?"

"Good, good. He went with me to Birmingham for that course on Internet analysis a couple of weekends ago," Janice said. "Our first trip away together."

"Birmingham." Roach wiggled his eyebrows. "Romantic."

"It's nicer than you think, these days," Janice said. "Plus

my grandparents live there, and Nanna always did insist on meeting my boyfriends before I was allowed to get serious about them. So I killed several birds with one stone."

Roach smirked as he took a sip of his drink.

"And did he pass the Nanna test?" Graham said as he walked up with a bottle to top up their glasses.

"Oh, she *adores* Jack," Harding said. "He fixed her computer, figured out how to lower her gas bill, and then took her shopping."

"Nailed the audition, then," Graham said.

"Never in doubt." She grinned.

Graham imagined the intelligent and articulate Wentworth charming Harding's octogenarian grandmother, a woman she'd described one night at the Bangkok Palace as "Not so much 'pre-internet' as 'pre-electric,' with a short fuse to match."

"Yeah, I can imagine that," Graham smiled. "He's got style, that Jack, the kind of style that nannas appreciate. And how was the course?"

"Oh, pretty good. There's a lot to learn and things are changing faster than anyone can keep up with. But if we get hacked, I should know how to track the hackers down."

"Terrific," Graham said.

Barnwell was regaling Roach once again with the story of how he narrowly averted tragedy on the battlements of Gorey Castle. "He was all set to do it," Barnwell told him. "I could tell. His stance, you know, the way he'd placed his feet. He was getting ready to push her. Right where that young groom died a while back."

"Exact same spot," Graham testified. "That would have been just *too* much. Besides, I'm not sure poor Stephen Jeffries would have made it through another murder investigation at the castle. While he must have nerves of steel and the patience of Job to be an events manager, I think he'd rather face a thousand bridezillas and their mothers than go through that again."

"And he doesn't want his business being the center of attention for all the wrong reasons. I think we can all understand that," Janice said.

"Mrs. Taylor's in the same boat," Graham agreed. "There are still people who visit the White House Inn as part of a 'murder mystery tour' or something. They do all the usual tourist stuff – the zoo, the castle, the old German tunnels – and then they stand outside the White House Inn, gawking at the window of the room where that murder victim stayed."

"It's the people that set up these tours that I blame. It's nothing but voyeurism," Harding said. "Exploiting tragedy for a quick profit."

Graham shrugged. He'd long since given up trying to understand this aspect of human behavior. "We've always done it, and probably always will."

"Speaking of quick profits, I had to go out to warn off a French boat the other day." Barnwell embarked on another story describing his most recent trip into the unpredictable waters of the English Channel. "So, the Coastguard gets this call from one of the locals, saying there's a French-registered vessel within a few minutes' sailing of the Jersey fishing sector, right?" Groans of unwelcome familiarity met his words. There was a three-mile exclusion zone around the coast of Jersey, jealously protected by the island's fishermen. Attempts by French fishing boats to encroach upon it brought storms of angry protests and occasionally, volleys of rotting fish. "I got hold of them on the radio, but they refused to leave the area," Barnwell was saying. "So the rulebook says I have to head out there with the Coastguard and see what's what."

"You're also entitled to whistle up the Navy if things get really unpleasant," Roach said.

"Well, no one wanted to go that far. I guess the Coastguard thought the uniform and a pair of broad shoulders," Barnwell added with a self-confident grin, "would help me successfully deal with them."

They all nodded. The size of the fish stocks and their impact on the livelihoods of the local fishermen and the broader Channel Islands economies were the common denominators behind these low-level conflicts. Further, the situation was compounded by a strong dash of patriotism or xenophobia, depending on ones' viewpoint. It didn't help that the French fishermen regularly came ashore, an act that appeared to be designed to rile the locals. All the Gorey officers had been called out more than once to calm down some Anglo-French argument that had manifested itself after one too many pints down the pub, a leer in the wrong direction, or a sneaking suspicion that the visitors catch was more sizeable than legally possible.

"How is the new Coastguard commander to work with?" Graham asked. "Ecclestone, right?"

"Yeah, he was brought in to replace Murphy a month or so ago. Prickly customer, I'd say. He was working on the mainland but was reassigned down here. And rather suddenly, so I believe."

"I rather expected him to come to the station to introduce himself. Was he at least helpful?"

"Sure," Barnwell said, "when he wasn't yammering away in French on his phone." Barnwell rolled his eyes. "Something about his brother and a surprise party. His sister-in-law is French, apparently. On and on he went.

Then he told us all about what a fantastic life they lead in the South of France and what a great country France is to live in, blah, blah, blah. I got the impression he was showing off. You know, sounding *cosmopolitan* so as to impress us plebs. All it did was put my back up. And he needs to keep his trap shut. He'll have the locals revolting if he's not careful with all that pro-Froggie stuff."

"Sounds a right charmer," Graham said. "Can't wait to meet him. What happened in the end?"

"Oh, the men on the boat threw their hands up and blamed their navigation equipment. Didn't believe them, of course. It beggars belief in this day and age. We're all carrying around GPS devices on our phones. We couldn't get lost if we tried, and yet these guys managed to be *seven miles* off course, and just *happened* to be inside the three-mile zone. Ecclestone wanted to confiscate their equipment, but I wasn't in the mood to ruin someone's livelihood. They didn't look like they were doing too well as it was. I didn't see a single fish onboard," Barnwell continued. "Anyhow, we ran alongside them for a while, exchanged a few, ahem, words, and when they got the message, shepherded them out of the area. I just hope they took the warning seriously. Next time, I will call the Royal Navy. They're always happy to enliven a trespasser's afternoon without getting *too* punitive."

"How did the locals react?" Graham hazarded a naval metaphor. "Did they call for them to be strung up from the yardarm?" For a man who lived on an island, he was woefully ignorant about the blue depths that surrounded him.

"Yeah well, I told a few of the guys about the ear bashing I gave them, and they seemed happy enough. Word will get around that we're on it."

"Good lad," Graham said. "That three-mile limit is like a sacred contract. There's nothing more likely to anger them than encroachments upon it, and the last thing we need is the fishermen up in arms." The list of potential public order issues in Gorey wasn't a long one, but rioting fishermen – fearing for their jobs and angry at the French, the European Union, the British government, and inevitably, eventually as their front line representatives, the Gorey police – was right at the top.

Graham turned to listen as Roach took Harding through the tricky questions he'd navigated as part of his sergeant's exam. "I think I had to memorize about a hundred new crimes and every recent Act of Parliament. I thought my head was going to explode."

"But you're staying in Gorey," Harding wanted to confirm, "even though you're an illustrious sergeant, now?"

Roach gave a laugh. "Where else would I go? This is home, and I couldn't imagine working anywhere else." This was a departure for Roach. Before Inspector Graham's arrival, Roach had wanted nothing more than to climb the career ladder on the mainland, preferably at the Met. Now, it would seem, he had all the excitement he craved right here on Jersey.

"And what about you, sir?" In the glow of the party to honor him, Barnwell felt confident enough to ask Graham, "Do you think you'll stay, now you've become a local hero, cleaning up the crime rate and everything?"

Graham waved away the characterization. "It's *you* they're impressed with. I just facilitate." He noticed the door of the lobby crack open. A familiar face appeared. "Marcus!" he called, stepping out into reception and waving him in. "Grab a drink, and let's toast the royal success of the good constable." Graham stood back to let the older man pass by into his office.

Marcus Tomlinson, the local pathologist, had a different look about him from the one he normally wore. He seemed vaguely harassed, his appearance just slightly askew. Today, his sky blue necktie looked to be on a journey of its own. "Phew, it's blustery out there. I'll be glad when this weather settles down and all we have to contend with is non-stop rain. Thank you, David." He accepted a glass of port. "And well done, Barry. You're a credit to the force." Barnwell shook his hand.

Graham took Tomlinson aside. He wanted an update on Roach's work in the crime lab in St. Helier where the sergeant was seconded three mornings a week to assist with forensics work. It had been six weeks since he had started. "Have you heard how Jim's doing at the lab?"

"First rate," Tomlinson replied. "They haven't let him do anything too dangerous or sensitive yet, but he's observed some of my post mortems, and he's learning the ropes very quickly. Natural scientific mind, that lad."

Graham felt yet another surge of pride for his diligent, hard-working officers. He had soon formed the opinion that it would be a tremendous waste for Jim Roach to spend decades noting down the details of missing bicycles or booking in the rowdy drunks following Saturday night alter-cations. His was a mind too fine and sharp for such drudgery, and this arrangement with Tomlinson and the Jersey SOCO team now seemed one of Graham's better ideas. In truth, he'd have gone to almost any lengths to help further the careers of his three charges, and also to make sure that the increasingly indispensable Jack Wentworth had plenty of opportunities to demonstrate his talents on behalf of the Jersey Police force.

Jack was the last to arrive, and Graham couldn't help noticing the genuine affection between the young computer engineer and Sergeant Harding. "Good to see, isn't it?" he remarked to Tomlinson as the pathologist helped himself to a second glass of port.

"Hmm?"

"Janice and Jack," Graham clarified. "They've really hit it off."

Tomlinson regarded the couple fondly. "Ah, young love," he sighed. "A path that never runs smoothly in my experience, but one well worth taking, wouldn't you say, David?"

The DI gave the older man a skeptical look. "I'd say it's a great thing when someone can see past the uniform, the pepper spray, and the powers of arrest to appreciate the thoughtful, sensitive person within."

"Preach, David."

"I'd also say that I'm proud of my officers, and I sincerely enjoy fêting their achievements, but I've got plans." He looked at his watch.

"Well, enjoy your evening, David. I'll make sure these youngsters don't get into too much trouble."

Graham found his jacket and was in the middle of texting Laura, the local librarian with whom he had a dinner date, when they all heard the reception desk phone ringing. For a few seconds everyone stared, until Jim Roach bowed to the inevitable and left the room to answer it.

CHAPTER THREE

HARDING AND GRAHAM arrived together, noticing at once the strangely subdued atmosphere in the pub. They found Tamsin sitting with one of the bar staff, a college-age girl who had the expression of someone entirely out of their depth. She looked relieved when Harding came over to their table.

"Ms. Porter?" Harding asked. Graham stood behind her, taking in the details.

"It's been seven hours," Tamsin said. Her face was puffy and reddened from an afternoon spent waiting in increasing distress. "He's never been this late before. Never," she ended simply.

Harding sat opposite her and began taking notes on her iPad, while Graham did the same with his trusty notebook.

"We've been in touch with the Coastguard," Janice said, putting her hand over Tamsin's and looking deep into her eyes. "What was his name, love?" The sergeant knew the missing man's name but asking his girlfriend to say it out loud was a gentle way to pull her out of her shock and into the present.

"Greg. Greg Somerville." Tamsin squeezed her eyes tight shut and pressed her hands between her knees. She tightened her shoulders briefly before relaxing them, sniffing, and opening her eyes.

"Why did he go out in his boat?"

Tamsin explained the project they were working on, and how Greg had to manually check the buoys at intervals. "We normally go out together, but he went alone today."

Graham kept a close eye on Tamsin throughout. Right now, this was simply a missing person callout. They were here to gather more information for the Coastguard. Nevertheless, he found himself attempting a rough mental calculation that would tell him how often someone had gone missing precisely because of the very individual who had *reported* them missing. Police work had made him preternaturally suspicious, and while, of course, everyone was innocent until proven guilty, it was also true that everyone carried the *potential* for guilt. His mind wandered to Laura who had graciously accepted his apologies concerning their dinner. She would, he knew, take a different position, her view of the human condition being far more trustful.

"What does the boat that he went out in look like, Ms. Porter?" he asked.

"It's a standard Warrior 175 small motor launch, white with a red stripe. *Albatross*. Basic model. The sea's a bit rough today, but nothing Greg couldn't handle."

"How do you stay in contact when he's out there and you're on land?"

"There's a VHS radio onboard, and sometimes we'll have phone contact. Before calling you, I contacted the Harbormaster and confirmed that Greg had checked in with him as he left. He was always punctilious about that. But we've heard nothing from him since. He left around noon and should have been back hours ago. On a bad day, doing the rounds of the buoys takes no longer than three hours." She reeled off the coordinates of the buoys that had been tracking the sharks' movements. "I've been here ringing and texting and trying to raise him on the radio, but there's been no response at all."

Graham walked outside and made several calls, including one to Barnwell, who was liaising with the Coastguard once more. "It's a Warrior 175 small motor launch, white with a red stripe." Graham described the position of the buoys Greg had been tracking, reading the information that Tamsin had given him verbatim from his notebook because he had no idea what it meant. "Get the word to them, all right? Sharpish, mind. He's been gone since noon. Should have been back four hours ago."

"If we find that the sharks are on their way to a mating location off Norway, as Greg predicted," Tamsin was saying when he went back inside the pub, "we'll be able to pressure the government to restrict fishing activities along their route and help keep them safe." In her shocked state, Tamsin was now sharing information irrelevant to the situation, but the police officers listened to her sympathetically, knowing that it was her way of coping with the fear that was enveloping her.

During the course of the short interview, Graham learned about shark migration, their breeding patterns, the detection of living things underwater, and the technical specifications of the trackers they had been using to monitor the sharks.

"And," Janice hesitated, anticipating the tricky question she had to ask next, "how did he seem in himself? Generally, I mean?"

"He's anxious about the research. We've been doing this

for three years now, and we need to start showing some results for our efforts. This is a make-or-break year, really. He was feeling the pressure."

"And how would you say he was responding to the stress?"

"By being irritable and taking it out on everyone, including me. Oh wait, he would never...no, no, that's not Greg at all. Definitely not. He wouldn't harm himself." Tamsin lifted her chin and for the first time during the interview seemed confident and in possession of herself.

"No medical history that might have caused an emergency?"

"No, nothing."

Eventually, Harding escorted Tamsin to her room and arranged for a doctor to visit and prescribe a sleep aid, if necessary.

"She's absolutely wrung out," Harding commented as she returned to the bar. Graham was making notes and occasionally glancing out of the window at the harbor. All the fishermen, including the stragglers, had been back for a while now, their lobster pots and fishing nets mostly full. The bar was filling up as a hard day on the water translated into a lively evening in the pub.

"For sure. She's had a rough afternoon," Graham said.

"What do you think, sir? Man overboard?"

"Probably. The Coastguard's been scrambled, and I've given Barnwell the buoy locations so they can focus their search. There isn't any more we can do." A grisly image formed in Graham's mind. "Wait a second. These... sharks. They're not *dangerous*, are they?"

A few moments' intensive searching on Harding's iPad yielded the reassuring fact that nobody had been attacked by a shark in British waters for many generations. "It's normally a case of mistaken identity," Harding explained. "The shark sees an object silhouetted against the surface, and bites it, just to see what it's made from. But Holden sharks don't feed like that. They filter the water like a whale."

"Okay, I'm with you so far," Graham said. "But these sharks," he continued. "They're big, are they?"

"Up to fifteen feet long," Harding marveled, showing the DI a picture. "Ugly brute, isn't he?" Although undeniably impressive with its massive, gaping mouth, the Holden shark had a curved, hooked, prehistoric shape born from millions of years of slow change in the silent deep. It was quite unlike the powerful, darting predators of the movies. This was a gentle, slow cruiser, much more like a whale, as Harding said, than the sharks of nightmares.

"Teeth or no teeth, a beast that size could overturn a small boat without even thinking about it." He imagined the scene. "The boat capsizes, and then begins to sink, leaving Greg alone in the water without a radio or even his survival gear."

"Terrifying," Harding agreed. The thought of being lost in that freezing, rolling water as night fell made her shudder. Optimistic by nature, she sought to bolster her spirits by searching for alternative explanations for Somerville's disappearance.

As she and Graham returned to the constabulary in their marked patrol car, she threw out every possibility besides "man overboard" that she could think of. She hoped her boss might latch onto one of them, but in truth, his mental processes remained as mysterious as ever.

"He could have just run out of fuel," Harding tried.

"Anyone who's ever been to sea before would carry extra, and check their tanks before leaving, surely. Besides,"

Graham argued, "he was only going a few miles from shore."

Harding kept trying. "Then, a mechanical problem?"

"One which wiped out his engine, radio, and satellite gear, all at once? Are we proposing that the vessel was subject to catastrophic, spontaneous combustion?"

Harding felt a little poked at. "Well, how about it?"

"Someone would have seen it," Graham explained. "From the third floor of the White House Inn, you can see most of the way to the South Coast on a good day. A fire would have stuck out like a sore thumb, even a brief one."

"Perhaps he found something fascinating or unexpected and is just chasing it down?"

"Without radioing anyone to relay his plans or his findings?" Graham countered. "And what could so engage his attention that he'd choose to stay out past nightfall?"

Harding shrugged. "Good point."

The DI glanced over at his colleague. "Sorry if I sound negative, Sergeant, but we're eliminating the possibilities and doing so very efficiently. My bet remains man overboard, and the longer he's gone, the more confident I feel I'm going to collect on that bet. Unfortunately," he added quickly before Harding could consider him hard-hearted.

"But," she added, "he could be on his way back, right now, with some story about a balky engine. Or maybe he just felt in need of some quiet time away from his responsibilities."

Harding pulled the vehicle into the small turning circle outside the constabulary. Graham glanced at the clock on the dashboard and stifled a sigh. It was now too late in the evening – yet *again* – for there to be much hope of spending any time with Laura. "If so, Sergeant, I would understand *exactly* how he feels."

They kept an altitude of around three hundred feet above the waves, forming a steady, figure-eight flight pattern in the pitch-black sky. Strong gusts of wind buffeted the sides of the helicopter, but it was holding steady. The search area was large enough to encompass the entire operational range of a seventeen-foot launch. If the *Albatross* was still afloat, they would find it, either from a radar return, or direct observation from searchlights in the helicopter's nose. So far, there was no sign of the scientist or his boat.

Commander Brian Ecclestone liked to sit up front with the pilot. This wasn't strictly necessary, as his responsibilities were chiefly to monitor their radar gear and coordinate with the two vessels below that were also combing the waters. That could be done from further back in the cabin, but being up front made Ecclestone feel "in touch" with events, and it meant he could pester the pilot about his fuel levels, the flying conditions, and other extraneous information not critical to their mission.

"You've been doing this a while, then?" he asked the pilot.

The younger man's eyes were glued to his controls, with the occasional glance outside at the deep, endless black of the sky. With little moonlight, and windy, overcast conditions, there was no real way to tell where the waves ended and sky began, so the pilot relied on his instruments to stay on course. "Since the army, sir," he replied. "Eleven years, altogether."

"Impressive," his boss replied simply. Ecclestone was too new and too incurious to have learned much about the crew he was working alongside. Besides the volunteers who made up a significant part of service, there were a dozen professionals who patrolled this stretch of water between England and France and who had dealt with everything from smugglers and people-traffickers to missing yachts and mysterious floating containers. They oozed competence, which left the comparatively bumbling, traditionally desk-bound Ecclestone feeling decidedly ordinary. So, consciously or not, the new commander felt the need to have his finger on the pulse of the service, placing himself as close to "the action" as possible. He glanced at his watch. "Sorry to keep you boys out so late."

From the mid-deck space behind him, the junior crewman had a standard response. "It's what we do, sir." His tone said the rest: *And we've been doing it perfectly well and for a long while before you came along.*

"Well, this guy owes us an apology, once we find him. A small vessel like that, in this weather? What was he thinking?"

The pilot had this one covered. "We prefer to blame the conditions, sir. Never the seafarer."

These were admonitions Ecclestone had heard before. His ponderously slow rise through the ranks had been punctuated by impolitic gaffes including a deeply unfortu-nate one the previous year. Ecclestone had been tasked with coordinating the rescue of a family whose motor-sailer had run into difficulties in the Bristol Channel. The rescue was nearly flawless, no thanks to Ecclestone's constant interfer-ence, but once the terrified family was safely aboard the rescue boat, he'd given them all a stern dressing down, complete with patronizing reminders about basic sea safety. Traumatized by his experience, and now enraged at having his children lectured on marine safety even as they sat, soaked and shocked in their life vests, the father of the family chose to make a formal complaint.

Memorably written on House of Commons notepaper, the missive came from Jacob Ellis-Dean, the veteran Member of Parliament who just happened to be the stricken boat owner's father. Partly due to this insistence from on-high, Ecclestone was judged "unusually insensitive and lacking in empathy" and reassigned to a less busy Coastguard station where his grating manner and selfish habits would cause less frequent offense. This story of his fall from grace found itself communicated, in humiliatingly rich detail, to every member of the Jersey Coastguard even before he had taken over as their commander and on his arrival at his new post, he found his team willing to do little more than tolerate him.

"Well, blame the weather all you like," Ecclestone was saying, "but people who go out unprepared are just plain stupid. And then we have to come out here and get them, in the middle of the night, when we'd all rather be doing something else. Right, son?" he asked the pilot, wisely deciding against nudging the young man with his elbow to elicit a response.

"Nothing beats flying, sir," the pilot replied. "Even at night," he said. "And for whatever reason," he added pointedly. "The poor guy might have drowned for all we know. His family, at least, deserves our best efforts. And besides, it's our job."

With that, they turned west again to begin another leg of their search pattern. Beneath them, the waves provided only dull, repetitious, unremarkable radar returns, and neither their searchlights nor those of the two vessels below them found any trace of Greg or the *Albatross*.

CHAPTER FOUR

J IM ROACH GRITTED his teeth and pulled hard
to open the heavy main door of the Gorey Constabulary building, fighting against the roaring gale that
had been building all day. He stumbled in, watched
by a bemused Barnwell who was manning the desk while
Roach – younger, but now a more senior rank – finished
another vehicle patrol.

"Flippin' heck," Roach said as he let the door slam and
shook off the first drops of what promised to be an awful lot
of cold rain. "It's *fierce* out there."

Barnwell handed his colleague a steaming mug of tea.
"Everybody got their hatches battened down?"

Roach took the mug with a grateful smile. "As far as I
can tell. I mean, you'd have to be living in a cave to have
missed all the warnings. First time in thirty years we've had
something like this. No one I've spoken to seems sure just
how bad it's going to get, so they're preparing for the worst.
Have they called off the search party for that scientist
fellow?"

"Yeah, they have." The two men were silent for a moment.

"Well," Barnwell said, stirring and reaching for a portable long-wave radio, for years his chosen method of listening to the cricket on the BBC, "let's get the latest, eh? I think we're right on time."

It was a phenomenon every bit as British as the changing of the guard at Buckingham Palace or the smearing of toast with Marmite. *"And now the Shipping Forecast, issued by the Met Office on behalf of the Maritime and Coastguard Agency at 1806 hours today. There are warnings of gales in Thames, Dover, Wight, and Portland."* The honeyed, contralto tones of the announcer were a calming contrast to the coming storms.

Roach shrugged. "They aren't kidding around. That's the whole south coast of England."

Barnwell nodded, listening carefully. "And the Channel, too. We're going to be right in the middle of this, Jim."

The BBC announcer continued the formulaic reading of weather predictions for the coming hours, describing each sea area in turn, clockwise around the country. The North Sea was angry, with winds of gale force eight and nine, but the predictions for the Channel areas were far worse.

"Thames, Dover, Wight, Portland. Southwest severe gale nine to hurricane twelve. Heavy, thundery showers. Poor, becoming moderate later."

Roach blinked a couple of times. "All right, that didn't sound good, but what did they actually say?"

Barnwell was already on the phone. "They said we're going to take a big hit tonight. Hurricane force winds, rubbish visibility, lots of rain and thunder."

Jim gulped. A once-in-a-generation storm wasn't something he'd ever prepared for. "What do we do?" he asked, already worried that he'd be out of his depth in this evolving, dangerous crisis.

"Well, the first thing to remember is —" Barnwell advised.

"Don't panic," Roach recited. "Always fantastic advice. I've lost count of how many times that saying has saved my bacon."

"And as for what to do," Barnwell continued, tapping his finger against the phone pressed to his ear, "I'll find out, as soon as the boss is good enough to answer his bloody —"

Click.

"Graham here."

"Evening, sir," Barnwell said, gathering himself quickly. "Bit blustery tonight, isn't it?"

"I'll say, I hope you're doing what I'm doing and staying inside." There was a growl in the DI's tone, a reasonable reaction to a work call during his precious evening hours.

Jim Roach grinned to himself at Barnwell's near *faux pas.* He could hear Graham's distinctive voice even from a few feet away, and he wasn't surprised to find his boss just as reluctant to wade into the middle of a hurricane as he was.

"Right," Barnwell said, making notes. "We'll follow the emergency plan, sir, and I'll call the Coastguard and stay in touch with St. Helier." Jersey's smart, re-built police headquarters would be the operational hub for the coming crisis. "Will you be in attendance, sir, if required?" he asked.

Roach heard Graham grumbling colorfully before assuring Barnwell that he'd be ready if the situation demanded it. His reluctance sounded almost total, but the two men knew that if Gorey needed his leadership and experience, even if it was just to provide an extra pair of hands, he wouldn't let them down.

"Okay, sir. We'll keep you updated." Barnwell replaced the receiver. "I have the sense," he said turning to Roach with a crooked smile, "that this storm may be seriously inconveniencing DI Graham's evening."

"His and everyone else's," Roach replied, "from Bristol to Sevenoaks and beyond."

Barnwell grinned again. "But I think our DI has...shall we say...*plans* for tonight, Jim."

Roach gave his colleague a look of shock. "Wait...You mean..."

"I do," Barnwell confirmed.

"But..." Roach began.

"He might work like a machine, but he's still a regular guy, you know," Barnwell reminded him.

"Wow. I never thought I'd see the day," Roach wondered, his eyes wide.

"We wouldn't be seeing it now, except for the arrival of our new librarian. I think the DI has been," Barnwell looked outside at the weather, "swept off his feet."

Roach continued to marvel at this turn of events, revising his view of DI Graham as a straight-up workaholic and contemplating for the first time the notion that his boss might have a *romantic* life. "Looks like he'll be able to relive that experience tonight, many times over," Roach quipped, following Barnwell's eye. "He can simply go outside. What did they say on the TV news earlier? 'Winds of a hundred miles an hour'?"

"And more," Barnwell told him. "We're going to lose roof tiles, windows, and maybe some boats in the harbor. Lots of flying debris, branches, and such. Flooding, too, I shouldn't wonder. We won't come through completely unscathed, so we all need to be ready to get out there and help, all right? It's an all hands situation."

Roach headed to the small police station's back room, a storage area where they kept uniforms and a small amount of special equipment. He donned waders and zipped up a heavy bright-orange rain jacket, flipping down the hood so that he was left with a letter-box size view of the lobby. He staggered back into reception. "I'll stay dry, that's for sure. Shame I can't see a bloody thing."

Barnwell brought out his phone and took a picture. "I'm going to call this one, 'David Against Goliath,' or perhaps, 'Jim Versus the Hurricane.'"

"What's that for? Posterity?"

"The Constabulary's Twitter feed," Barnwell chuckled.

Jim gave him a dirty look but headed back to find more foul weather gear for his fellow officers.

"Don't forget Janice," Barnwell called through. "She's out on the coast, but she'll be back in a minute." No sooner had he spoken than Janice bustled her way through the door, nearly tumbling into the lobby.

"Whose idea was this?" she demanded, shaking rain from her hair and rubbing her hands together to restore some feeling to her chilled limbs. "I know it's November, but I mean, for heaven's sake!"

"Hurricane force twelve," Barnwell announced from behind the desk. "It's going to get special around here."

"A *hurricane*?" Harding spluttered. "Marvelous. Can't wait to hear what the DI thinks about *that*."

Jim Roach returned from the back room with an armful of more brightly colored gear. "It could be one of Bazza's wind-ups, but according to him, the boss is on a *date*?"

Harding didn't show any surprise. She found tea and blew across its surface while cradling the mug with her freezing hands. "Laura Beecham, right? The librarian? Where've you been, Roachie? They're often in the Bangkok Palace on Friday nights."

Barnwell was shaking his head. "It takes all sorts."

"Why not?" Harding asked. "They're both single, she's attractive and educated, and he's... well..."

"Unique?" Roach tried.

"A strange, workaholic loner?" Barnwell added.

"Very eligible, I was going to say," Harding smirked. "I'm surprised this hasn't happened sooner."

Barnwell began monitoring the BBC's weather website, frowning at the latest radar map. It showed a huge mass of swirling clouds that obscured an area from Somerset, in southwest England, to Brittany, in northern France. He grumbled something and then returned to their discussion. "The DI works like his life depends on it. I'm amazed he's found time for a woman."

"Perhaps he works like a dog precisely because there's nothing else in his life," Roach interjected.

"When the right one comes along..." Harding began, but thought better of it. Their boss' romantic life was a remarkable novelty, but it felt churlish to gossip, not to mention intrusive. Besides, their small island was facing a grave threat, and the Constabulary was about to be dealing with its most serious public safety challenge in years. There were things to do.

The reception desk phone rang. "Gorey Police, how can I help you?" Barnwell said. "Oh, hello Mrs. Taylor, how are things at the White House Inn?" The constable listened for a moment and then began making notes. "Well," he replied, frowning, "I don't know if I can tell him *that*, in all serious-ness." Roach approached the desk, curious as to what Mrs. Taylor had to say. "No, ma'am, I'm afraid I can't pass that on...Not tonight," Barnwell twirled a pen between his fingers. "Why? Because we've a hurricane headed our way. Dealing with the serious public safety threat it poses is our priority right now. I don't think DI Graham'll have a lot of time for that kind of thing, not tonight, Mrs. Taylor." He put his hand over the mouthpiece and looked at the other two, raising his eyebrows, "If ever."

Harding mouthed, "What's up?" but Barnwell raised a finger.

"I can pass on your concerns, Mrs. T, but —" He listened as Mrs. Taylor continued for another few moments. "No, ma'am. I really can't ask him to come out for something like that. Not during the worst storm in thirty years."

Undeterred, Mrs. Taylor persisted until Barnwell eventually relented. "Okay, look. I'll tell him that you'd like to speak with him in person, and that it's important, all right?"

This seemed to placate the owner of the guesthouse, and she rang off. Barnwell took a deep breath before making another call to DI Graham.

"Sorry, sir. It's just that Mrs. Taylor has been calling, and she's...No, sir. There's no trouble over there, but she's got some concerns about...Yes... Would you, sir? I'd be very grateful." Then he added, "Er, stay dry, sir."

Barnwell grimaced as he replaced the receiver, ready for the ribbing his two colleagues would inevitably mete out. "Stay *dry*?" Harding queried. "In a *hurricane*?"

Barnwell shrugged. "Hurricane or not, he's headed to the White House Inn," he said, making himself another mug of tea. "And hopefully, he's taking his sense of humor with him."

CHAPTER FIVE

B Y THE TIME DI David Graham arrived at the
White House Inn overlooking Gorey Harbor, the
sky had transformed into a dark, brooding mael-
strom. The usually busy streets were empty with shops
already shuttered, and the White House Inn looked as
prepared for a hurricane as one might hope. The orna-
mental plant pots had been taken in and every one of the
guesthouse's windows was closed and taped. Out of habit,
Graham found himself glancing up at the second-floor room
that had been Laura's during her first weeks on Jersey. He
looked to see if the light was on. It wasn't. Laura had
quickly found a place of her own, a place in which DI
Graham had once again planned to spend this foul,
inclement evening until the call from Mrs. Taylor came in.

The guesthouse proprietor met him at the door and
then securely bolted it again as soon as Graham entered the
lobby. She seemed ill-at-ease, wringing her hands and
frowning. "Mrs. Taylor, I'd wish you a good evening, but I
really don't think we're going to have one."

"Come through, Detective Inspector. Thank you for coming."

She led Graham into the restaurant area and bid him sit down on one of the armchairs by the large picture window that in normal circumstances gave a broad view of the beach and sea beyond. This evening, it was impossible to see anything further than a few feet. The room was perhaps a third full with guests. November, coming as it did between the summer and winter holiday tourist seasons, was one of the quieter times of year. "I'm sorry to call you out in this terrible weather."

"It's going to be one for the record books," Graham reminded her. "Are all your guests aware of what's going on?"

"Yes," she replied confidently. "The staff has been getting everyone ready, and we're as hurricane-proof as I can make us. In fact," she added, "it's the hurricane I wanted to talk to you about."

Graham raised a puzzled eyebrow. "So how can I help you, Mrs. Taylor?"

She sat in the armchair next to him, leaning in as though confiding something sensitive. "I don't really know how to say this, but I need to give you a warning about the storm."

"I think the BBC has that covered, Mrs. Taylor," Graham replied. "The whole south of the country is taking shelter. They've canceled trains, directed people to stay at home, the whole shebang."

"No," Mrs. Taylor said, clasping and unclasping her hands. "No, there's something else."

Very unusually, Graham reached over and placed a hand on Marjorie Taylor's arm. "What's upsetting you, Mrs. Taylor? Are you afraid of damage? Because your insurance will cover all of the —"

"Nineteen eighty-seven," Mrs. Taylor proclaimed, sitting a little straighter in her chair. Graham removed his hand and sat back. "The Great Storm. Do you remember?"

Graham nodded. "Not really, I was too young, but of course, I've heard of it. Worst gale in living memory, wasn't it? Twenty-odd people killed, houses destroyed by falling trees, and an incredible mess the next morning. Precipitated by the BBC weatherman saying it wouldn't amount to much."

"It's what came *after* the storm that I need to warn you about," Mrs. Taylor said. She looked distinctly uncomfortable in her chair, almost squirming as she tried to get the words out. "Last time, in eighty-seven, there were some very strange goings-on in the days after the storm."

Graham said nothing for a moment. Investigators tended to view stories of "strange goings-on" rather like archaeologists might receive the latest theories about aliens building the pyramids. "What kind of strange things, Mrs. Taylor?" he asked patiently.

If anything, the guesthouse owner became even more agitated. Her hands were a tangle of knotted fingers, and she scowled at the tabletop in front of her as though angry at having to shoulder this burden alone. "Ever heard of Tony White and his son, Tom? They disappeared in eighty-seven, a few days after the storm, while at sea on the *Smart Alec*."

Graham confessed that he hadn't.

"Never found," Mrs. Taylor continued. "No evidence of their boats, no life rafts, no calls for help on the radio. Just *vanished*."

"You believe their disappearance was connected to the storm?"

Mrs. Taylor nodded, her expression dark. "I'm not

alone. Plenty of people around here thought there was something funny about it."

"But," Graham pointed out, "they were probably out in rough seas, weren't they? It seems perfectly plausible that the weather, just a few days after a storm of that magnitude or even a simple miscalculation could account for their disappearance. Seafaring is not an innocuous occupation, is it now?"

"No," she admitted, "but something... *unusual* was abroad during those few days, Detective Inspector. Something *awful*." She could see Graham wasn't convinced. "Well then, what about the tiger that disappeared from the zoo?"

Graham blinked at this sudden change of tack. He was familiar with the story of the missing tiger. It had passed into island folklore. On his only visit to Jersey Zoo, he'd been told how a Bengal tiger had gone missing during the 1987 storm. According to the zookeeper's telling, the striped feline roamed Jersey for three days, mercifully without harming anyone. "What about it? The tiger was found, Mrs. Taylor."

"No, no, no," she spluttered. "That's not true!"

Graham had a fondness for Marjorie Taylor. She had helped him settle into the community during his first few months, and he'd always respected the professionalism and discretion with which she ran her establishment. But now, he had the real sense that he'd been called away from spending what had promised to be a delightful evening with an intelligent and desirable woman, braving the opening salvoes of a hurricane in the process, only to listen to half-baked conspiracy theories. "Mrs. Taylor," he said, "a tiger has to eat enormous amounts of food to stay alive. We'd have had complaints from farmers, gamekeepers, and landowners that their livestock had gone missing. There would be tracks, distinctive paw prints, unmistakable fur left tangled in barbed wire...This would have happened regularly for years. It wouldn't be hard to track a full-grown tiger on a place like Jersey."

Mrs. Taylor powered on, apparently undeterred. "Well, how do you explain the sightings?"

Graham ached for a cup of tea. "Sightings?" he managed to ask.

"Tony White and his son. People have seen them in the churchyard and on the beach late at night. Two ghostly figures, hovering above the ground," she described. "And Mr. Croft saw the 'Beast of Jersey' while walking his dog across farmland just this last summer."

The Detective Inspector found himself on the verge of a withering tirade. How could an experienced business-woman like Mrs. Taylor possibly lend credence to such claptrap? The sighting of a tiger was in reality most likely an overgrown housecat and ghostly apparitions the result of too much imbibing down at the pub. He was never more grateful to hear the sound of his phone vibrating in his pocket. "Excuse me, Mrs. Taylor," he said. He returned to the quiet of the lobby.

"Sir?" It was Barnwell.

"Constable, you do realize I've battled a storm and wasted a good chunk of my evening in order to hear ghost stories and other such rubbish from Mrs. Taylor?"

"Yes, sir," Barnwell said. "Sorry about that."

"And now, I imagine, you're going to make it up to me by telling me I can relax for the duration of the rest of the evening?" Graham asked, more in hope than expectation.

"I'm afraid not, sir," Barnwell confessed.

"Why am I not surprised?" Graham closed his eyes. "Okay, let me have it."

"We got a call from your old friend and mine, Mr. Hodgson," Barnwell said.

"Ah yes, the seventeen-year-old boy with a penchant for nighttime sailing excursions," Graham remembered at once. "I hope he's hunkered down at home tonight."

"He's fine," Barnwell said, "but he claims his grandparents have refused to comply with the coastal evacuation order."

The problem laid itself out for Graham like a maze seen from above. "Why do I have the feeling I'm about to get involved in this?"

"The fire brigade is swamped and can't get there for another couple of hours. They requested that we attend."

Graham blew out his cheeks and tapped his foot. He looked around, making sure that Mrs. Taylor and her guests were thoroughly out of earshot, before telling Barnwell precisely how he felt about his suggestion.

"Right, sir," Barnwell said, moving quickly past his boss' very negative rejoinder. "Shall I meet you here at the station, then?"

"Very well," he sighed. "I'll see you in ten." He looked outside at the weather. "Maybe fifteen."

After he'd ended the call, Barnwell turned to Roach, who was still dressed from head to foot in luminous foul-weather gear, and said, "I honestly don't know which will prove worse tonight – the hurricane, or the DI's temper."

Laura glanced at the clock yet again. It had been forty minutes since David had left, putting dinner – and the rest of a relaxing evening – abruptly on hold. She was becoming anxious about leaving the lasagna in the warm oven for so long. The pasta would dry out. Inherited from her Italian grandmother, the recipe was completely foolproof, so long as hurricanes and unwelcome police duties didn't interfere. "Hurry up, David," she found herself muttering at the clock. "I'm hungry."

The librarian poured herself another small glass of Cabernet Sauvignon and turned the oven temperature down yet again. There were *antipasti* laid out, so far untouched. She spooned homemade mushroom caviar onto a cracker. Outside, the wind had picked up and now sounded a noisy lament around the tiny cul-de-sac where Laura had been fortunate enough to find a small, affordable place to rent. The larger bedroom had a view of the fields beyond the edge of Gorey, while the diminutive window in the smaller upstairs room showed the very edge of Gorey Castle looming over the village from its imposing cliff-top perch.

As early as 3 PM, Laura had helped to hurriedly close the library, and then retreated to her small cottage where she and Graham had planned to endure the storm and get to know each other a little better. "Finally," she had smiled to herself. Since her return from a two-week stay in London, where she had been a vital witness for the prosecution in a high-profile, armed robbery trial, thanks to the Detective Inspector's numerous commitments, they'd managed to spend only three evenings together. Their relationship was developing terribly slowly.

"You're an enigma, David Graham," she'd thought during their second date. More than any man she'd ever known, Graham had proved to be endearingly inscrutable. He didn't evince any particularly strong political views, he was dedicated to his work but shy of discussing it outside of the station, he clearly cared about his subordinates beyond their shared profession, but was reserved in his expressions of affection, and more than anything, she was struck by his discretion when it came to his past. Over several hours of conversation, Laura found she'd learned almost nothing about his life before Gorey, except that he'd been in or around London, solving crimes and ascending the promotional ladder faster than he'd expected.

Somewhere along the way, she'd concluded, his wheels must have simply fallen off. The break with London was too sudden and complete to be caused by anything inconsequential. He had left behind his friends and family, his professional contacts and the beats he'd covered for years, all to live in one of Britain's true backwaters. *Why would a seasoned detective abandon the big city and come to live somewhere so very, very quiet?* she had written in her journal after that fascinating, frustrating second date.

"You are a puzzle," she now said to herself, sipping her red wine. "But really a rather good-looking one."

The phone rang. "David?" she asked.

"Hi," he said, rather sheepishly. "I'm the guy who was planning to have dinner at your house a hundred years ago. I wonder if you remember."

She smiled, pleased to hear his voice. "I think I do. Is the lasagna going to be released from the oven any time soon or are there further offenses to be taken into account?" She heard him sigh, and knew the evening was a bust.

"I'm sorry. I'll tell you about it later, but for now I have to go tie a rope around my middle and rescue a couple of pensioners from their own home before they drown."

"Oh, that's a shame! But oh well, I understand. My

hero!" she finished, mustering some enthusiasm from some-where. "Please be careful. It looks *awful* out there."

"It truly is," Graham confirmed, "but the fire brigade can't do it, so I won't be able to relax until I know…"

"I understand." Laura knew this was the time to be supportive, just as he'd stood resolutely by her during the stress of the trial in London. He'd talked with her four or five times a day over the phone, reassuring her and making the whole experience a lot more tolerable. "Take care, okay?"

"Depend on it," he promised her. "I'll phone you as soon as I can."

As Laura ended the call, the strongest gust of wind yet seemed to catch her home with a thunderous broadside. Laura moved over to the kitchen wall where a fireplace had once stood. It was the thickest in the house, and it made her feel a little safer. Through the noise of wild gusts of wind, she heard a tentative knock at her front door and after a moment of hesitation, she moved to answer it.

"Billy! What're you doing here?" Billy Foster was her favorite library visitor. Insatiably curious with a passion for all things related to space and astronomy, the nine-year-old visited the library at least three times a week. His mother was just out of rehab, and he'd gone back home to live with her, but Laura could tell from his increasing visits to the library that things were a little rocky.

She bundled the boy inside. He was drenched from head to foot. "Take off your jacket and your socks and shoes and go and sit in front of the fire in the living room to keep warm. Oh, and ring your mum, tell her you're safe. Tell her you'll stay here until morning."

She grabbed a towel as the boy shuffled off and joined

him by the fire, kneeling down next to him. "What were you thinking, Billy? Going out in this weather."

"I didn't think it'd be this bad, miss. I've never seen rain like it," Billy said as Laura roughly toweled his hair.

"No, well, none of us have, Billy."

Billy looked over at the table. "Having someone for dinner?"

"I was, Billy, I was."

Billy, being a nine-year-old boy, didn't ask with whom Laura had been planning to have dinner. Instead, he sat silently, his head buffeted by her ministrations as much as any hurricane.

"There, I think you'll do." Laura sat back and looked into Billy's big, trustful, innocent, hazel eyes that were framed by fair, almost white eyelashes. They'd seen a lot in his troubled, short life. She took his hand. "Billy, would you like some lasagna?"

CHAPTER SIX

ET APART FROM Gorey by a stretch of sloping farmland, the tiny coastal community where the elderly Hodgsons lived was almost lost amid the sheeting, wind-blown rain. There was a group of six houses, only one of which had any lights on. "There they are," Barnwell told his boss, as they pulled up in the patrol car. "Should just be the two of them, according to young Hodgson."

"Great," Graham told him. "Can we get any closer, do you think?" An S-shaped gravel driveway led from the country lane down to the house, and Graham enjoyed not at all the thought of wading laboriously through floodwater to reach the stubborn seniors who lived there.

"Sorry, sir," Barnwell said. "If we flood the exhaust system, or if water gets in the fuel lines…"

"Okay, Constable," Graham said. They were both wearing rain gear, but Graham knew he'd end this expedition soaked, freezing, and miserable. Barnwell, on the other hand, seemed positively enthused to be tackling a rescue attempt in these dreadful conditions. "Lead the way, lad,"

Graham said. "Just turn if you want to say something, so I can hear you, okay?" It was a trick from times long past and half-forgotten, learned in conditions even worse than these.

"Right, boss." Straining, they levered open the car's doors and managed to squeeze themselves out into the ferocious gale. A second later, both doors were slammed closed by windy hammer blows that shook the whole car. Barnwell shouted something his grandmother would have clipped his ear for, and led Graham along the sodden driveway toward the house. The water was past their ankles, cascading down the gradient from the farms that lay inland. Powerful enough almost to knock Graham off his feet, it was an angry, freezing torrent whose only desire was to race headlong into the Channel beyond.

Barnwell turned to his boss. "Get the rope tied on, sir," he shouted over the gale, offering Graham the end of a short line that was already secured around Barnwell's waist.

"We'll be fine," Graham called over.

But the junior officer insisted. "No rope, no rescue," he yelled. "Now please, sir." Barnwell helped Graham get the rope tied, their freezing fingers finding the sodden line hard to handle. They pushed toward the house. Lights were on, both upstairs and downstairs, but in the pouring rain, they shone no brighter than a faltering match.

"What happens," Graham asked as they struggled their way forward, "if they're absolutely adamant they want to stay?"

"It won't matter. They're coming with us, sir, no question. If the water gets worse and takes out a load-bearing wall, they're done for. We'll arrest them if need be." In recent months, Barnwell had built a reputation as something of a daredevil, and given his experience in dangerous situations, was showing he had the confidence to take *de facto* operational control.

"Okay," Graham said simply. He'd have given a month's salary for a Jersey Coastguard helicopter to relieve them of this loathsome responsibility. While they were about it, they could give him a ride back home, preferably to Laura's front door. But it wasn't to be.

Barnwell reached the cottage first, tugging the rope so that Graham joined him. They sheltered under the battered wooden awning that flapped ferociously above the doorway. "Well done, sir," he said. "Now, let's get them out. Holler like you mean it." The two men pounded on the door and yelled, "Police! Mr. and Mrs. Hodgson!" a half-dozen times before they heard the metal clicking sounds of the door being unlocked.

"Oh, hello!" Mrs. Hodgson said brightly, lightly brushing windblown hair from her face. "It's the police, Albert," she called back, rather unnecessarily.

"The police?" an elderly male voice replied, walking along the hallway to be greeted by the sight of two sodden officers at the door. "Whatever is the matter?"

Barnwell barely restrained himself from rolling his eyes at Graham. "Didn't you get the warnings?" he demanded. "There's a bloody hurricane on the way. Evacuation orders are in force for this part of the coast."

"Evacuation?' Mrs. Hodgson marveled. "Surely not."

"No ifs, ands, or buts," Barnwell told them. "You've got ninety seconds to grab some personal belongings, and then we're off."

Albert Hodgson took a couple of steps forward. "Can I get you lads a cup of tea?"

Graham swallowed the urge to arrest him on charges of "sheer lunacy," and "recklessly endangering a spouse." "I don't think you understand, sir. It's hardly the time for tea. We've got to get you to safety, *fast*."

Albert laughed. It boiled Graham's blood in an instant. "Safety?" the old man chuckled, thumping the cottage's substantial, stone walls. "This place is a strong as the Coliseum. I hate to have wasted your time, but we won't be going anywhere."

Graham swore under his breath. "Right. Time to crack the whip," he muttered to Barnwell.

"This isn't a discussion," Barnwell told the Hodgsons sternly. "We're leaving, immediately, all of us. Do you have good boots or wellies? We can't bring the car any closer. We'll have to walk up the hill." Graham glanced back. The car was completely invisible behind icy curtains of rain, blown to an acute angle by the roaring gale.

"You're welcome to spend the rest of the storm here," Albert offered, as though he hadn't heard anything the officers had said. "We've got that baking show on the TV, and there's plenty of tea in the pot."

Graham felt Barnwell's hand on his shoulder. "Action Plan B, sir. Back me up, all right?" Without another word, Barnwell leaned down, threw two huge arms around Mrs. Hodgson's soft, ample waist and hauled her bodily onto his shoulder. "Time to go," he said simply. He turned and began carrying the startled woman through the rain, up the hill.

"Shall we?" Graham asked Albert, who was watching this turn of events open-mouthed. "Constable Barnwell takes public safety very seriously," he explained to the elderly man with a wry smile. "Grab your boots and let's go."

When Graham told the story days later, he compared the sight of Barnwell hauling Mrs. Hodgson to safety to watching King Kong man-handling a woman to his mountain lair. Only, Barnwell managed to do it all while climbing a slope, keeping his footing on loose, flooded gravel, withstanding the outrageous force of the wind that threatened to flatten them all, and ignoring the distressed pleas of the rain-soaked Mrs. Hodgson.

"Left leg, right leg," Graham called back to Albert, now tied to him by the same rope with which Graham had been attached to Barnwell earlier. "Everyone's at the church hall in Fenton," he shouted. "Plenty of tea. And I believe they *also* have the baking show on the telly." Somehow, Graham found, this actually motivated the tiring Albert Hodgson, and within a few minutes of commencing Barnwell's Plan B, they were at the patrol car.

"Never in all my life!" Mrs. Hodgson was still complaining. "Of all the indignities! I never thought I'd ever —"

"You're welcome," Barnwell said, guiding her into the back seat. "Now, if you'd be good enough to pipe down, I'll get on the radio and see how things are." Graham made sure Albert was buckled in next to his outraged wife, and with Barnwell behind the wheel, they made their way slowly through the sheets of rain and roaring wind to Fenton church hall. It was normally only a ten-minute drive, but tonight it took them half an hour. Once the Hodgsons were safely ensconced and unlikely to escape now that they had tea and cake and the ear of other locals who listened with rapt attention to the tale of their rescue, Graham called Laura while Barnwell radioed the station.

"Mission accomplished," Graham said proudly. "I'm sorry it's so late."

Laura tried, and narrowly failed, to stifle a yawn. "Heroics take time. The man of the hour needs... well, a little more than an hour, but I understand," she told him. "It's okay. Hopefully there won't be another hurricane *tomorrow* night, and we can try again."

Graham sighed with disappointment out of Laura's earshot, but managed to keep all of the night's various emotions out of his voice. "It's a date. Let me dry off, and I'll call you tomorrow."

"Please do," Laura said, and bid him goodnight.

CHAPTER SEVEN

T HE FOLLOWING MORNING, the skies were grey, the weather squally, but the raging winds of the previous evening had moved on to punish the Atlantic, where the hurricane's force would inevitably peter out as it moved north to colder climes. On the beach, Sergeant Roach surveyed the damage left behind with a furrowed brow. Not in the living memory of Gorey had their seafront come under such a powerful and sustained assault from Mother Nature. The disarray was a stark and unpleasant contrast with the usually neat, traditional feel of the place. Hardly a square foot of sand was absent some form of debris, and a small army of volunteers and Community Support Officers – uniformed, but without the powers of arrest – were laboriously cleaning up the sad mess.

"Now then, James," said Roger Percival, a fifteen-year veteran CSO with whom Roach frequently worked on those busy weekend nights when the locals got a little too drunk and rowdy, "isn't this a thing?" He gazed with Roach over the beach, scattered with branches, plastic trash and old nets long since turned green and slimy from years on the open water. He zipped up his jacket all the way to the top, the better to protect himself from the wind that still swirled, chilled and damp.

"It's not pretty," Roach admitted, "but at least no one died. You know, the hospital at St. Helier went into full emergency mode, but all they had was a couple of lacerations from flying glass, and one elderly man treated for shock."

"We can all be grateful for that," Percival agreed. "The thing now is to make the place shipshape again. Care to join me?"

It was a running joke between them – Roach was as hands-on as any officer on Jersey – and the two grabbed thick, black, plastic trash bags and began scooping up rotten wood and nameless debris with gloved hands and metal pickers normally used to collect litter. To Roach, it appeared their comely, much admired beach had been unsuccessfully stormed by an army of old trees, their casualties now strewn around, broken and forlorn.

"I see your lot got your names in the *Gorey Gossip* again. Have you read it yet?" Percival asked, relishing the chance to rib his senior officer.

Roach grumbled, shoving a weary-looking length of netting into his trash bag. "DI Graham told us to take a professional view of such publications," Roach told him. "And as for what he wrote about last night's operation, Mr. Solomon can take a running jump off the docks, for all I care. Just provided he waits for high tide."

Percival got a good laugh out of this, and he spent the next few minutes revisiting (mostly for Roach's benefit) the excoriating post that local man, Freddie Solomon, had published on his scandalous, salacious, and ceaselessly popular blog. "'Like the Three Stooges caught in a hurricane, except there were four of them," the CSO quoted from the article about the Constabulary's response to the previous night's storm. "'Ineffective disaster management by a bunch of bumbling idiots with all the professionalism of a—'" Percival delighted in the retelling, but he stopped when he saw the look on Roach's face.

It was one so stern and unimpressed that Percival fell silent. For a few minutes, they gathered debris without speaking, finding a severely battered old lobster pot, and to the bemusement of both, a scarlet negligée, now faded to a baby pink by a combination of sun and salt. "I'll guess this made its way over from France," Percival surmised, holding it up between the jaws of his picker. "I'd say plenty of folks enjoyed staying in last night 'n' all," he chuckled.

Roach's thoughts flashed briefly to the Detective Inspector and the speculation around his supposed relationship. Roach liked Laura. She was personable and smart. He couldn't imagine the DI choosing anyone whose mind was not as vibrant as his own. He gave a little smile and hoped the hurricane hadn't ruined the couple's evening entirely.

But then, Solomon's irresponsible and dishonest blog began to truly bother him. How could the Constabulary be accused of being unprepared? Warnings had been issued, no one had been seriously injured. Vulnerable members of the community had been contacted with plenty of time to spare, and if necessary, escorted to safety. Barnwell had pulled off another of his impromptu rescues down at the Hodgson's, right on the coast, for heaven's sake.

"I'd give us an A-minus for last night," Roach said, feeling the need to defend their small team. "We all worked our socks off to keep everyone safe. The DI was out until all hours, helping Barnwell get people to safety, and liaising with the fire brigade about the flooding."

"Commendable," Percival allowed, digging up another length of partially buried old sea rope. "Crikey, this thing's older than I am," he marveled. "Amazing how long things stay intact, what with the sun and the saltwater. You'd think they'd be long gone." He manhandled the rope into his trash bag and moved on, side by side with Roach, along the beach. "I don't think that Solomon fella's fair in the slightest," Percival shrugged. "But he's very *readable*."

"So are comics," Roach retorted.

"The thing is," Percival continued, undeterred by Roach's obvious distaste for Freddie Solomon's sub-tabloid level "journalism," "he always seems to get the scoop before anyone else."

"Hmm," Roach said neutrally.

"Remember 'The Case of the Missing Letter'?" Percival asked. He put up his fingers to make air quotes.

Roach paused. "You're being rhetorical, right?" he asked. Percival, unsure as to what "rhetorical" meant, gathered the word's meaning from Roach's demeanor. He, and much of the island in general, knew that Roach had been a central figure in bringing that complex case to its conclusion.

"Sorry, I forgot. You were heavily involved, weren't you?"

"I am familiar with the case," Roach added, sounding as though he was gritting his teeth.

"Well, young Freddie knew about that all-important letter, long before your lot figured everything out," Percival said. "And before even the great DI Graham."

Roach was tired, his smart uniform boots were covered in wet, dirty, storm-tossed sand, and he could have done without needless allegations of incompetence or unjustified digs at him or his colleagues. It wasn't true that Freddie knew about the letter, but "truth" didn't seem to be an unquestionable underlying principle as far as Mr. Solomon's writings were concerned. Rather than give the usually affable and helpful Percival a piece of his mind, Roach did as he felt the DI might do. "And was the murderer arrested, tried, and convicted?" he asked.

"She was," Percival allowed.

"And has that been the case with every suspicious death on the island since DI Graham arrived?" Roach pressed.

Percival was forced to concede that it had. "A solid record, one would have to say."

"Then," Roach added, letting his temper seep into his voice just a fraction, "what say we ignore Mr. Solomon's half-baked rubbish and concentrate on *this* mess instead?" he said, motioning to the wind-blown beach. As he waved his picker in the air, his eyes caught on something in the distance. Something that he knew was out of place.

"What is it, Jim?" Percival asked, alarmed at how the younger Sergeant had frozen in place.

"I'm not sure, Roger. But I'm going to find out," Roach said, his eyes fixated on the sight far down the beach. He started to walk away from Percival before increasing his pace to a sprint as his legs carried him across the beach seemingly at a rate that rivaled the winds of yesterday's hurricane. Something was most definitely not right.

The boat's engines ceased their noisy rattling as Hugo Fontenelle pulled off his headphones and reduced the throttle to idle. "Ready, *Messieurs*?" he called back to his two colleagues. "At least we have better weather than yesterday, eh?"

Far enough out that they could only barely discern the Jersey coast to their south, the three-man crew of the *Nautilus* were relieved to be at sea again having beaten a hasty retreat to land the previous day on account of the storm.

"Ready," Victor Delormé growled in French. The much older man, a hopeless chain smoker, hunkered over the battered suite of electronics equipment, checking the connections and ensuring that data would show up on his small, green monitors as soon as the dipping sonar became active. "Lower away."

Suspended from a hastily constructed rig, the semicircular, metallic dome of the sonar unit began its long fall. Mechanisms whirred above their heads, letting out strong, metal cable, as the dome splashed into the water and headed down at a rate of a foot each second. Its speed increased as it plunged, leaving the disturbed, surface water behind and passing through the cooler, calmer thermocline and into the depths of the English Channel.

"Below the layer," Victor reported. "Temperatures are low, but nothing we didn't expect." The hurricane had, in Victor's words, "done a number" on the Channel the night before, upturning the careful balance of dense, salty water and lighter, fresh currents. The weather had thrown the two into direct conflict, creating a dynamic, underwater seascape.

"Not too fast," Hugo reminded him as Victor reached for the mechanism's speed lever. Hugo was a slight man, bespectacled, privately educated, barely out of his twenties, and unused to the sea. He had spent his first days out on the water battling seasickness, his moans and lassitude trying the patience of the other two men on this voyage to the point that they questioned the wisdom of their decision to join him. "We don't want the current to catch the cable and whip it around," Hugo said.

"Yeah, we know," Jean-Luc Bisson, a rugged, handsome man in his late thirties said, pushing his thick, black hair off his face. "We've done this before, you know. Relax and let us work."

Their unlikely, three-man partnership was born of necessity. Hugo had the funding to mount such a speculative expedition, while for Victor and Jean-Luc, both experienced deep sea divers, this chance for a few days' well-paid work was as welcome as the start of the Bordeaux wine season, and that was before they considered the "bonuses" their work might bring forth.

Beside the sonar device, Hugo had bought a range of second-hand gear from salvaged fishing boats, and even some old, surplus French navy equipment from the gray market. The *Nautilus* itself was a remarkable salvage and repair story, a trawler given up for scrap, but which, with a cautious initial investment and much hard work, had been resurrected. She was a lumbering, often uncomfortable boat, but there was enough space for their electronics and other gear, and the hull was tough enough for most conditions. Except, of course, those of a full-blown hurricane.

"Want to try the magnetometer?" Hugo called back to Jean-Luc, who was observing the diminutive green screen with Victor. Both stared in hopes of a favorable reading, but beyond typical background scatter from the seabed, they saw nothing.

Jean-Luc rolled his eyes, but casually turned around to focus on his own area of responsibility. According to the scuttlebutt and rumors that abounded around Cherbourg Harbor, Jean-Luc was "curiously gifted" at his task. He used a method that had remained basically unchanged since his grandfather's day; a small, sophisticated, torpedo-shaped device towed slowly behind the boat, poised to indicate concentrations of ferrous metal by their telltale, if absolutely tiny, magnetic fields. "Nothing yet," he called back. It was rather like metal detecting on a scale writ large.

Hugo had the job of piloting the boat, making deliberately slow headway along the figure eight patterns he'd laid out on their charts. It was the classic approach of a team looking for something.

Each of the three found themselves enthused and cautious, by turns. They would have admitted that their main impetus for this unusual expedition was dockside rumors, some of them going back many generations, and most of them spurious. However, Hugo's argument had always been that as the rumors hadn't been disproved, they could be true. To the others, who were older and more seasoned with extensive experience of the sea's capricious nature and the romantic stories that abounded from it, this sounded like fanciful, wishful thinking. If, however, they located their quarry, the payoff would be nearly incalculable. Certainly enough, as Jean-Luc had reflected that morning, to fund a nice villa by the beach on the south coast of France. It was his retirement dream, and to achieve it, all they needed was one strong, incontrovertible signal from their equipment.

"Anything?" Hugo asked, trying to appear authoritative and seaman-like. Both older men shook their heads. "Maybe a school of herring," Jean-Luc told him. "But nothing like what we're looking for."

"*Merde,*" Hugo swore. "This was as likely a spot as any," he added, almost to himself. He stepped forward to lean over Victor's shoulder. "*Mon Dieu.*" A pile of damp, discarded cigarette butts surrounded the feet of the chair upon which Victor was sitting. Several were now stuck to Hugo's shoe. Unusually for a Frenchman, he did not share Victor's love of Gauloises and wrinkled his nose in disgust.

"You always tell us this," Victor complained. "That this place is 'likely,' or that over there is 'a good possibility.'" Victor stood, towering at least a foot over the leader of this expedition, whose hold on that position was tenuous at best given his dependence on the two more experienced men.

"The only proof of how likely a spot is, will be the ping of the magnetometer," Jean-Luc explained, in a careful tone, "or a big green mass on the sonar screen. Without those, each place is as fruitless as the ones before." The two men hunched over their equipment again, their point made. Hugo stared at the unresponsive backs of their heads before returning to the boat's pilothouse.

Victor and Jean-Luc would not tolerate optimism for its own sake. They were too tough, too hard-bitten, to take anything for granted, and too knowledgeable to accept encouragement from someone with far less experience, even if he was paying them. Neither would be content nor would their moods improve one iota, until they held their cherished prize in their hands. Only then would they know that enduring the risks this search posed and the potential derision of their fellows back at the docks of Cherbourg had been worth it.

CHAPTER EIGHT

FREDDIE SOLOMON STROLLED along Gorey's main shopping street feeling pretty good about the world. He'd long since learned to ignore the odd glances cast at him, confident in his belief that "no publicity is bad publicity" and was gleefully unselfconscious in his checked, flannel pants and jaunty cravat. He had the air of someone who had just learned an embarrassing secret about a person but had chosen to keep it to himself for the moment. Amid the uniformity and conformity of Gorey locals during this off-season, he was a surprising splash of color, both in attire and personality, and the traditional, conservative community was still divided about whether or not Freddie Solomon was entirely "a good egg."

"Morning, Gracie!" Freddie chirped as he passed an elderly woman in the street. These encounters had become a useful measure of Freddie's impact, and a good barometer of his readership. Initially, he was skeptically ignored or frowned on, but more recently, his online writings had finally begun to garner consistent public attention. Readers of the *Gorey Gossip* considered themselves well informed, and if Freddie chose to spice his reportage with a pinch of hearsay or a soupçon of speculation, then it just made it all the more entertaining.

Gracie gave him a twinkling smile and tapped the side of her nose with a forefinger. It had become the "secret signal" among Freddie's growing cohort of senior informants; people who enjoyed his blog, his colorful character, and the thrill of self-importance he bestowed on them as a result of their association with him. This group of co-conspirators was well-placed to unearth tidbits of gossip from friends, family, and neighbors and was willing to toss what they'd learned on to the pyre of unchecked facts and sensationalism that comprised the writings of Freddie's blog. Freddie had already characterized the mysterious deaths that had occurred since Graham's arrival as a "spate of murders," a representation that the DI and his fellow officers found to be a gross exaggeration. As a source in Freddie's one-man investigations into the personal aspects behind these deaths, Gorey's retired community was a goldmine.

When the Granny Grapevine went quiet, or had yet to receive news of a particular event, Freddie resorted to his back-up source for hot tips; an expensive police scanner of questionable legality that provided up-to-the-second intelligence and enabled him to ascertain information within seconds of it reaching the hands of the police. Being quick-footed and with loose professional and personal boundaries, he was able to report on this information quickly, on some occasions *before* the police, wrong-footing them and removing their advantage in the process. Needless to say, he was not looked upon kindly by DI Graham and his officers.

This time, Gracie had nothing for Freddie save a

promise to keep her ear to the ground, so he sauntered onward, down to the bottom of the hill where the old post office, two gift shops, and a classy, fine bone china tea room flanked the narrowing street. Steps led down to the board-walk, which in turn led either to the marina, mostly empty of working boats at this time of day, or to the broad, sandy curve of Gorey's much-loved beach. It was just as he set foot on the sand, hoping to see for himself the fruits of the labo-rious clean-up operation that had followed the hurricane and to which he had not contributed a single ounce of effort, that he heard a passer-by utter words that thrilled him from head to toe.

"Old Frank at the Harbormaster's office reckoned he washed up last night."

Freddie turned smartly to follow the meandering couple, a woman in her fifties and another who might have been her daughter. He began listening with a single-minded intensity.

"Poor lad," the younger woman was saying. "Have they any idea who it is?"

Freddie crossed his fingers in the hopes of learning more. A real-life *corpse* washed up on Gorey beach would provide at least a thousand words of good, *titillating* copy.

"Remember that young scientist? The one looking for sharks. He didn't come back in the day before yesterday. Word is that it's him."

Freddie almost jumped with excitement. He was, of course, familiar with that missing person case, and he had already been asking questions around the pub and the marina hoping for a juicy story perhaps involving corrup-tion, professional rivalries, or maybe some prurient details about a relationship gone awry. Now, and he barely stopped himself from rubbing his hands with glee, he had confirmation of a tragedy, a circumstance for which he was particularly suited. Freddie felt that he was gifted at expressing the unspeakable in those heartfelt and human moments when people were at their lowest and most likely to talk about a loved one, especially to a sympathetic stranger who showed great compassion while interjecting an expertly timed, incisive question.

Peeling away from the ambling pair, Freddie began accelerating down the beach. He passed the decorative benches that lined the promenade, pulled up the collar of his tweed jacket against the inclement wind that came off the water like it meant business, and was soon faced with a cluster of people, a police car, and an ambulance, but, Freddie was delighted to see, no media people were yet in attendance. He'd have first shot at this story, out-maneuvering the workaday journalist hacks who were unlucky enough, and unenterprising enough in Freddie's opinion, to work for traditional news outlets.

Six people were standing around the body, which did indeed look exactly as though it had washed up during the night. It had come to rest on a small rise about ten feet from the concrete wall of the promenade. Freddie could see that the deceased was still wearing his shoes. He knew from his ceaseless research that this almost certainly ruled out suicide, but little else was visible through the crowd of legs and past the green bags of medical gear brought by the ambulance crew. He moved in closer.

"Do we know his identity?" Freddie asked anyone who was listening. He had the confident, full-throated voice of someone who knew his rights and would vigorously defend his having shown up somewhere he really oughtn't have.

"Step back, please, sir," said Roger Percival, the Community Support Officer. He was looking the part in his hi-visibility vest and neat uniform, grateful for a respite from the coastal cleanup but cold enough to hope that his part in this local emergency wasn't going to take too long. "This isn't a pleasant sight, and we need to give the attending officers room to work."

Such warnings were like catnip to Freddie. He took two or three surreptitious photos, feeling a familiar explosion of adrenaline, moving quickly and discreetly to avoid police censure. He would post them on his blog as soon as he was done here. Depending on whether his photographs went viral, he'd be in danger of being sued by the family of the deceased, but such risks thrilled him, and he was never slow to set aside moral scruples in favor of shooting unforgettable images. It was that *color* he most wanted to capture; that pallid, alabaster skin tone which spoke of a life forever gone and of a story just beginning.

Freddie asked a few more questions before being shooed away by Percival and the ambulance crew who were waiting for Marcus Tomlinson to arrive. Already drafting an article on his phone while he walked away from the scene, Freddie remembered another of his favorite refrains. It was borrowed from the mindset of every irresponsible, rushed, speculative journalist. It was one he was guided by, especially on those rare occasions when he was, just slightly, checked by some doubt as he prepared to hit "send." He didn't need to remind himself of it today, however. The sensation of the moment was enough to carry him through. Freddie Solomon was on his game. The thrill of the hunt, the story, was for Freddie, his life force. Now was the time for a pulsing journalistic thrust forward in the name of ground-breaking news coverage.

Then his would be the glory. *Publish or perish.*

CHAPTER NINE

The Gorey Gossip
Wednesday, November 14th

Tragedy struck our community today. It could have happened anywhere, but fate decreed that this misfortune should befall the town of Gorey. The body of thirty-one-year-old Greg Somerville was found at 12:30 PM, washed up on the beach around a half-mile from the base of Gorey Castle, a place with its own recent, blood-spattered history.

For those who knew and respected the young scientist, this is a day for shock and a week for mourning. For the rest of us, naturally upset at this unfortunate loss, Greg's death brings a contemplation of mortality and the infinite, but also important questions about this poor man, and how he met his untimely end.

We know that Greg was working for the UK Environmental Agency, involved in potentially dangerous work with large, migrating sharks. But having seen Greg's body with my own eyes this morning, I can testify against his demise having resulted from a shark attack; there were no bite marks, and Greg's body was pale and lifeless but entirely intact.

Instead, we must analyze other possibilities. I was shocked to see that Greg had suffered a devastating wound to the back of his head. From my own research, this wound appears consistent with the effects of a large hammer.

How might this unassuming research scientist have come to harm? Could there have been an accident at sea? Did someone wish to harm him? Why have there been no sightings of his small motor launch, the *Albatross?* Why did he not return the day before the storm? And what should we make of the behavior of his partner and confidant, Tamsin Porter? She was seen killing time in the Fo'c'sle and Ferret while her brave man was at sea, the day before the hurricane. Why did she not accompany him, as usual?

And if he was attacked, who would have lurked out in the Channel, ready to accost a lone, unarmed man? Could Greg have run into human-traffickers or drug-runners?

Found himself in the wrong place at the wrong time?

I have been roundly critical of Gorey Police on this blog, but now is the time for the beleaguered constabulary to take the lead and show that they can keep the good people of Gorey safe from harm. The circumstances of this young man's death must be vigorously investigated and those who perpetrated the crime brought to justice.

CHAPTER TEN

G RAHAM WAS READY for Harding's mild objection. "I appreciate that she's in a state, and she's had a rough forty-eight hours, but would you get her down here as quick as you can?" He was torn. The Greg Somerville missing person case had become a coroner's investigation, but until Tomlinson confirmed foul play, he could only gather background details. The DI had a firm sense that Tamsin had not yet revealed everything she knew. He hoped a more formal interview here at the station would yield more. "Thanks, Sergeant. See you shortly."

Before interviewing Tamsin, however, Graham felt obliged to spend a few noisy and instructive moments with Freddie Solomon. The DI slid his cellphone back into his jacket pocket and turned to face the blogger.

Freddie was sitting stiffly upright in Graham's office, looking around slowly at Graham's sparse collection of memorabilia and two awards set in small, glass cases. There was a picture of a group of young men, surely only cadets, in blue uniforms, and a framed newspaper front page featuring three mug shots and the headline, "Got 'Em!"

"I don't mind journalists," Graham began, pacing his office and loosening his tie as though this were a convivial chat and not the lecture both knew it would be. "In fact, we rely on the media to get the facts out about a case, descriptions of people we're searching for, and so on. I've had many an occasion to buy a journalist a drink for being mindful of the importance of open communications. We like to work hand in hand with the media. You scratch our back, we'll scratch yours, know what I mean?"

"Prudent behavior, all round," Solomon agreed.

"But you," Graham continued, his tone still level, "are *not* a journalist, Mr. Solomon. I'm not sure if the Internet has yet invented an appropriate term for just what it is that *you* are."

"I'm a *citizen* journalist, Detective. A journalist of the people."

Graham glared at Solomon. The little blighter seemed almost fragile, willfully foppish, but conspicuously unperturbed by Graham's manner. "You could be Citizen Kane and you still wouldn't have the right to drop me two ranks. It's Detective *Inspector*, Mr. Solomon," he rasped. "That's a detail you might find important to include in your *ridiculous* blog."

Solomon remained frustratingly impassive. "I'm not here to interview you, Detective *Inspector*. You called *me* in, remember?" he intoned. "But since you mention it, you'd be an interesting subject for a profile piece." Solomon stood, a half-foot shorter than Graham and side-eyed the inspector for a moment. "Oh, yes. Lots of complexity behind *that* grizzled exterior. A wealth of professional achievement, I'm sure. But controversy, too." He leaned in to whisper, "There always is."

Graham took a step back and allowed his anger to dissipate. "Mr. Solomon," he said almost mildly. "I'll be asking you to remove yourself from my police station shortly, but before I do, I'd like to offer you some advice." Graham looked down to make sure the little squirt was listening. "Interfering with police investigations, by which I mean," Graham clarified, "commenting on injuries to a victim, possible causes of death *and* spurious theories not grounded in any fact about likely suspects, before the police have cleared that information for release, is dangerous and *prejudicial* to our inquiries."

"It's my right, and my responsibility," Solomon reported.

Graham bit back an unprofessionally stern response. "It's 'perverting the course of justice.' Isn't that a marvelous old expression?"

"It's a beauty, but I won't be perverting anything. You can rely on my discretion." It was a bald-faced lie, and they both knew it.

Graham frowned at him like an unimpressed schoolmaster. "I bet I bloody well can," he growled. "Now, if I see details of a suspicious death, or anything else I don't like in your half-baked rant of a blog, we'll meet again. Only this time, you'll be in a jail cell downstairs, and I'll be writing you up for endangering the security of a police investigation. Do you understand?"

"I do," Solomon replied at once. "I apologize if I have over-stepped my bounds, Detective Inspector," he said.

There was a hint of flippancy in Freddie's tone that grated on Graham's last nerve and he took the slighter man by the shoulder. For a quarter-second, Freddie wondered if he were about to feel the DI's fist break his nose. "Come again, lad?"

"Nothing, nothing." Solomon held his hands up. "I'll be going."

"Indeed, you will," Graham said, shepherding the blogger out. He watched Solomon find just enough of a strut to effect a graceful exit and then took ten long, deep breaths as he stood in the silent reception area.

Barnwell arrived as Graham was exhaling for the tenth time. "Things that bad, sir? Or are we going for enlightenment?"

"Just bracing myself against the inevitable, Constable. Anything from the harbor?"

Barnwell frowned. "The rumor mill is working overtime, sir. Everyone is talking about the death. The natural assumption would be to assume that Somerville hit his head and then drowned, the vast majority of disappearances at sea do end just like that after all, but some of the fishermen are dreaming up a story that our victim was attacked. Nothing else makes sense, according to them. But you know how it is, they don't have any evidence, just 'a feeling.' None of them noticed anything unusual beforehand or at any time at all, so they reckon."

Shaking his head at this lively creativity, Graham said, "Where do they get this stuff?"

"The prevailing theory is that French fishermen are trying to stake their claim on Jersey's waters and Somerville's death is 'a message.' It's a ridiculous conspiracy theory if you ask me, but they're not happy people down there at the marina. They're unbelievably angry about the new fishing quotas the government has slapped on them, and tensions are running high with the usual anti-French feelings boiling over even more than usual. The Frogs don't help themselves by coming ashore, drinking, and eyeing up the women, of course. You'd think they were deliberately trying to wind the locals up." Barnwell rolled his eyes. "The local boys get territorial, and even if Greg Somerville's death turns out to be a simple drowning, the mood at the harbor is making me worried."

Graham's memory flipped back a few pages and showed him an article that he'd read in the local paper regarding tighter restrictions on the species that could be fished around the island. "Fish stocks need time to recover, but I understand their frustration. If they're not making money from the fish, the entire island economy falters. Everyone suffers," he said with a sigh. "No sign of Somerville's boat, I suppose?"

Barnwell shook his head. "Not a trace."

"Keep an eye on the men, okay? We don't want things getting overheated and some kind of vigilante action occurring." Graham suppressed a shudder. "Hopefully we'll get some information from Tomlinson soon that will take the wind out of their sails and things will calm down of their own accord."

"Will do, sir. I saw that pillock of a journalist on my way in. Did you skewer him without me? It was him who started these ridiculous rumors."

Graham allowed himself a satisfied smile. "All dealt with. I think there'll be a noticeable change in the tone of his blogging," he predicted. "And let's not legitimize what he does. He's not a journalist. He's a rumor-monger and a creepy, lying, little sh—"

"Right-o, sir. It's amazing how he finds these things out. How do you reckon he does it?"

"Probably consorts with other rats down in the sewers," Graham mumbled to himself. Barnwell chuckled at the idea, but turned his attention to work as he followed Graham's gaze to the station door. "We've got the victim's girlfriend coming in. Harding's with her, and I'll join them when they arrive," Graham said.

Barnwell returned to the reception desk just as the phone began to ring. Graham heard him get ready to patch the call through. "Dr. Tomlinson, sir," he called over.

"Excellent." *Click.* "Marcus. What have you got?"

"Well," the pathologist replied, "I've just finished Greg Somerville's autopsy. My estimate for the time of death is sometime on the day he disappeared, in other words, before the storm. The length of time he was in the water and the atrocious conditions confuse matters, but that's my best guess. The cause of death was blunt force trauma. He was hit around the head with something heavy and dull."

Graham sagged in his chair. "Oh, lord. Murder, then, for sure."

"I'm afraid so," Tomlinson confirmed. "We're looking at a deep, non-linear fracture of the skull about two inches in length. I can't be sure what weapon was used," Tomlinson admitted. "The wound had a very distinctive shape, like he was hit twice, or maybe once with a double-ended weapon."

"He didn't drown, then?"

"Definitely not. There was no water in his lungs. He was already dead when he went in the water."

"Well, that's something, I suppose." Graham thought for a moment. "Couldn't he have got stuck out in the storm and injured himself on the boat? Are you sure it wasn't an accident?"

Tomlinson didn't have to mull this over. He'd been as thorough in this autopsy as in any throughout his long career and had considered accidental death as well as homicide. "He has a number of wounds that are consistent with a struggle. The water washed away any evidence though, I'm afraid. Now, could it have been an accident? It's theoretically possible," he admitted, "but that wouldn't explain the scratches and bruises on his arms, and he would have had to have fallen quite specifically on something that caused this odd shaped injury. Was there anything that could match his injuries on board?"

"We don't have the boat. We've got people out looking for it, but nothing yet. And even if we find it, I suspect the effects of the storm will have carried anything loose on board to the bottom of the Channel."

"Yes, you're probably right, there. No, it's my considered opinion that it wasn't an accident, David. His injury was devastating, he would have died instantaneously. I have no doubt we're looking at a murder."

Outside, Graham heard a car engine cut out followed by the sound of doors slamming.

"Tell me, if he was attacked, do you think a woman could have done it?"

Tomlinson looked up at the ceiling of his office and squinted, "With the element of surprise, the instability inherent on a boat? It's possible."

CHAPTER ELEVEN

J ANICE AND TAMSIN bustled their way through the lobby doors. There were dark circles under Tamsin's hooded eyes, and she walked slowly to the interview room, guided by Janice.

"Can I get you a cup of tea, love?"

Tamsin nodded and settled herself at the table, forcing her hands down into her jean pockets. Janice closed the door and walked over to the filing cabinet that acted as a tea-making station. Her heart was heavy. If she were in Tamsin's position, Janice was quite sure she would barely be able to stand upright, let alone have pointed questions fired at her in the austere surroundings of a police station.

"Constable? Sergeant?" Graham called from his office door. "Join me for a moment, would you?"

The pair came into his office, and he shut the door. "The Somerville case is now officially a murder investigation. He was hit on the back of the head and died instantly, dead before he hit the water." He looked at Janice and pointed in the direction of the interview room. "Ms. Porter is now a suspect."

"Really, sir?" There was mild objection in Janice's voice. It was true that most murders were committed by people known to the victims, and that close family and friends were often the first people to be interviewed, but she found it hard to believe that the pale, shocked woman she'd just put in the interview room had killed her boyfriend. Still, Janice knew she was identifying too much with Tamsin and needed to put her personal feelings aside. She had a job to do. "Yes, of course. I'll make her tea and get her settled, then I'll run a background check."

"While we're on the subject of computers, could you do something for me, Sergeant?" Graham relayed the concerns Mrs. Taylor had regaled him with the previous evening. "She's certain that the '87 storm caused some mysterious...*vortex*," he said, his face apologizing for the term, "which caused some strange incidents and unfathomable, to her at least, disappearances. She's worried that that's going to happen again this time. Can you track down anything *odd* that happened during the week after the Great Storm but which later proved to have a perfectly reasonable explanation? Don't spend too long on it, just enough to show Mrs. T. that we've followed up and that there's nothing to be concerned about, that there's such things as coincidences, accidents, and mysteries that might appear extraordinary at first blush, but which are ultimately proven to have explanations that don't have their basis in hauntings, beastly threats, or other supernatural phenomena."

"I didn't think you believed in coincidences, sir."

"I'll make an exception in Mrs. Taylor's overly-imaginative case."

"Yes, sir." Janice bustled off to make the tea. Graham turned to Barnwell.

"Sit down, would you, Constable?"

Unsure as to quite what this invitation would lead to, Barnwell took a seat opposite his boss who was absent-mindedly turning in his swivel chair. Barnwell knew that this was another "thinking tactic" Graham had developed, not unlike those crazed scientists who summoned their best ideas when sitting in an odd position, upside down, their limbs awry.

"The woman in the next room," Graham began, clearly following his own train of thought and obliging Barnwell to serve as a sounding board, "is petite, not particularly strong, and apparently of sound mind. Yet, I'm about to question her in relation to an unsolved death. She's our prime suspect at this juncture."

Graham's eyes were glued to a patch on the wall. "Janice and I went through all the scenarios we could think of just after Somerville was reported missing. Listed all the potential reasons for his disappearance, eliminated those that were too wacky, and in the end, we, I, felt that an accident was the most likely explanation. Now Tomlinson says we're looking at murder, one that unusually happened at sea. Who would have gone to that much trouble?"

"Someone who knew how to navigate the water. Perhaps someone who followed him out there or came upon him?" Barnwell suggested. "Someone who might know where his tracking devices were located?"

"Hmm."

The constable picked up a pencil that lay on Graham's desk and twirled it between his fingers, like he'd seen the DI do, warming to his ideas. "In my experience, sir," he said, "people tend to end up dead because of money or love."

"Do you believe there's such a thing as a 'criminal',

Barry?" Graham asked as he continued to stare at a blank space on his office wall.

"That'd be someone who commits a crime, would it, sir?" Barnwell asked, as if suddenly concerned that the definition of the word had changed, and no one had told him.

"Normally, yes. But I'm talking about something deeper. A hereditary trait, or a deep-seated psychological characteristic. Something that *makes* someone a criminal, something that they are almost compelled to act out, making them different from the vast majority of law-abiding people."

Barnwell caught on quickly. "You're asking whether someone is capable of murder, sir, like from birth?"

"Hmm. And do you think we can, *should*, spot these people before they commit a crime?"

Following exactly the lessons his boss had passed on during previous months Barnwell answered, "I think it is better to examine the evidence at hand, sir, rather than make...how do you say? Subjective decisions."

His boss' occasional forays into psychology and even philosophy with respect to police investigations were apt to sail right over Barnwell's head. When Graham had arrived on the island, he had started with a policy of smiling and nodding at these musings, but more recently, he found himself turning the DI's gems of wisdom over in his mind at night. Even if he was still bamboozled by most of what Graham put forth, Barnwell thought about the Detective Inspector's ideas more than he would care to admit. And like his fellow officers, he admired Graham's remarkably keen mind.

Graham nodded his head toward the interview room. "You want to step in there and interview Ms. Porter?"

"Sir?" Shaking his head with unmistakable firmness,

Barnwell answered, "Well above my pay grade, sir. I'll leave the detecting to the detective, if you don't mind."

Graham looked at Barnwell, reminding himself how much fitter and more *together* the constable looked compared with a while back. "I'm not one to bother people about career progress and such," Graham said, "but I do hope your talents find a broader outlet than Gorey, some day anyway. Don't forget to challenge yourself, son. Move out of your comfort zone."

"For the moment, sir," Barnwell said, rising, "there's plenty to challenge me around here."

Unsurprised at Barnwell's unwillingness to take a professional risk, but not deterred, Graham let the matter drop for now. He picked up his notepad and a big mug of tea, and headed for the interview room where Tamsin Porter was waiting. "Ms. Porter," he began, setting out his notebook and taking a seat opposite her. "We're grateful for your time."

"Yeah, sure," she said. Her voice was weak, and she was pale, clearly badly shaken.

"I hope you'll accept our condolences. I'm very sorry for the way in which you found out the terrible news. That really isn't how we prefer to do things."

Ordinarily, it would have been Janice's job to notify Tamsin of her partner's death, but the *Gorey Gossip* had pre-empted even that courtesy. Tamsin had learned about her loss online, along with everyone else. She'd barely spoken since.

Graham employed his softest tone. "I'd like you to take me back to that morning, in the pub, before Greg left," he said.

Tamsin cleared her throat, dabbed her eyes once more, and began to tell the story of her last conversation with

Greg. Graham took notes despite the mandatory video camera in the corner, and simply waited. He felt sure that eventually, if she were guilty of anything, she'd say just a little too much.

But fifteen minutes later, it was clear this interview wouldn't be as straightforward as he hoped. Tamsin was being truculent. After relaying her recollection of the hours before Greg had left to go out to sea, she had only given the briefest responses to Graham's questions. He was frustrated, he wanted to uncover the truth, and this paucity of detail was alerting his suspicions. For her to be numbed by grief and shock was quite understandable. But to be deliberately terse and taciturn while investigators puzzled over her beloved's fate seemed decidedly odd behavior.

"You mentioned earlier that this was a make-or-break year for your project. That Mr. Somerville was feeling the pressure. Was this project going well? Was he getting the data he wanted?"

"Pretty much."

Graham rolled his shoulders. "Could you expand on that, Ms. Porter?"

Tamsin pushed her hands deeper into her pockets. "We play a long game. It's what we do. We stay persistent over years, looking for trends, patterns. And we go where the data leads us, at least we should. A good scientist would never force the data to support a hypothesis, just as you, I presume, would never make facts fit your theories of who was responsible for a crime. And so 'getting the data he wanted' isn't really the point."

Graham opened his mouth to correct her rather defensive interpretation of his question, but Tamsin continued. "Greg wanted to prove his hypothesis correct. I felt he was overinvested in it. That's a lot of what we argued about."

She sat up and twisted her body in the chair, her hands to her face. The pain that telegraphed itself in her posture and that which was etched in her expression was impossible to ignore.

The knock at the interview room's door was entirely unwelcome, but Graham knew that the case might develop quickly. "Excuse me for just a moment." He left the room and nudged the door closed, finding Barnwell outside, a troubled expression on his face. "Problem, Constable?"

"Yes, sir. I'm afraid there's something kicking off at the town council meeting."

Graham blinked for a moment and tried to visualize the scene. "The monthly meeting?" He remembered seeing the announcement in the local paper. "Kicking off?" Gorey's council meetings were hardly known for outbreaks of violence, or indeed anything out of the ordinary. They typically took less than an hour, and even public debates were orderly, taking place before an audience of no more than five in his experience. "Who started it?" Graham was immediately keen to know what might have so exercised such a mellow, unspectacular group.

"Des Smith, sir. He's on his feet, right now. Two different people called the station within moments of each other. They're concerned, he appears inebriated."

"First a hurricane, then a scientist shows up dead, and now I've got an angry, liquored-up salty seadog to contend with. Didn't someone tell me this was the 'quietest backwater in the British Isles?' What a load of...poppycock." Graham paused, looking back at the earnest expression on Barnwell's face. He stood silently waiting for direction.

"Well," Graham said, with a big sigh, "if he's risking a disturbance of the peace or might hurt someone, we need to deal with it. See you in the car, Barnwell." Graham went to conclude his interview with Tamsin.

"I'm, sorry, Ms. Porter, I've been called away. We will need to reconvene at a later time." He turned to Janice who was looking at him wide-eyed, surprised. "Would you please escort Ms. Porter back to her lodgings, Sergeant? We'll talk again soon," he promised Tamsin, "Tomorrow. Please don't leave the island in the meantime." He left the room abruptly, leaving Tamsin staring down at the table, slouching once more in her chair, her hands again shoved in her pockets.

CHAPTER TWELVE

BARNWELL DROVE THEM to the town hall at a brisk pace.

"How did the interview with Ms. Porter go, sir?"

"It would have been a lot easier if a certain someone hadn't published every last detail before we had even notified her of the death," Graham complained. "She wasn't very helpful, but I'm not sure if she was shocked by her loss and the method by which she found out about it, or if she was being obstructive on purpose."

"Annoying little blighter, that Freddie Solomon," Barnwell agreed. "But, 'freedom of the press' and all that. Got to tread carefully."

"But he's stirring things up," Graham sighed. "Getting folks riled up when there's just no information or justification for it. And that's before we get on to his callousness and his prejudicial treatment of the facts."

The converted church hall which served as the town council's venue was unusually busy with people milling around outside. As the two police officers approached, someone in the small crowd recognized Graham. "Evening, Detective Inspector," they said. "Suppose you're here about old Des, then?"

"Just checking things out. How long has he been going?"

The local man screwed up his face as he thought, then looked at his watch and counted quickly under his breath. "About twenty minutes now, I'd say."

"Quite the orator. What's he so angry about?"

"Quotas," six or seven people said together. Then one added, "Bloody unfair, they are."

"The fish probably wouldn't agree with you." From time to time, Laura flirted with vegetarianism and had been prompting Graham to consider it too, but he had found the resulting prohibition of full English breakfasts to be entirely unacceptable. "Well, let's just see how he's getting on," Graham said.

"Good luck in there, sir," someone called.

"Think we should have brought the riot gear?" Graham asked Barnwell, raising an eyebrow. The constable met his boss's glance and thought for a second, "We don't have a complete set, sir. Just bits and pieces. I'm not sure there's even one entire set on all of Jersey. Never been any need for it."

"There's always a first time."

Graham heard the harangue before he saw it. Drinks and snacks were laid out on the table in the small lobby, and through the glass of another pair of doors, they could see the tall, slightly bent figure of Des Smith, one hand aloft, giving someone his thoughts in no indirect manner.

"You've dealt with Des before, haven't you?" Graham asked quietly as they looked on through the doors.

"A few times. There were those break-ins down at the

harbor that time. His boat was one of those burgled by the Hodgson boy. And he had a couple too many, maybe three Christmases ago, and had to spend the night at the constabulary bed-and-breakfast."

Graham smirked. "I trust he found our accommodation to his liking." A jail cell at Christmas sounded like a grim way to spend the holiday.

"He's a bit of a firebrand. Old union leader, as leftie as they come. For years, he's been at the center of protests against quotas, the French, the government, you name it."

"So this isn't just a grievance about fishing quotas then, but the stirrings of a Marxist insurgency, eh? What else will this tiny town conspire to conjure up?" They watched Des' wild gesticulating as he continued his tirade for a few more moments. They could see the members of his audience bobbing their heads in agreement.

"If he sees you here," Graham wondered, "will he get angrier, or accept that his little monologue is over and wrap up?"

A shrug was his answer. "Could go either way, sir."

"We'll just let him know we're here, all right?" Graham pushed the door open and entered quietly before standing against the back wall of the hall. The room was fuller than any previous council meeting Graham had ever seen. Almost a hundred people were there, occupying every seat. Graham and Barnwell stepped around the left side of the hall and hovered on Smith's right flank.

A man the size of Barnwell, in full police uniform, was hard to miss, and Smith noticed him at once despite his obvious drunkenness. "Oh, aye. Here's the law!" he announced. "Come to take me away, then, Barry?"

Barnwell stood up tall, arms folded across his chest, feet apart. He felt a hundred pairs of eyes suddenly on him.

There were grumblings and a couple of complaints about the police having 'nothing better to do.' In his less conspicuous suit, Graham avoided this level of scrutiny, but nonetheless, they were vastly outnumbered, and theirs was not a comfortable situation.

"Just keeping the peace, Des," Barnwell replied. "Don't let us interrupt you."

Smith most certainly didn't, and revitalized, he continued to reiterate the difficulties facing his friends and fellow mariners in the fishing fleet. "Fish don't just jump out of the sea all by themselves, you know? Someone has to go out and get 'em. People forget that. They don't give a thought to how they come to be on their supermarket shelves or in their fishmonger's cold cases. It's a hard, dangerous way to make a living, fishing is, one that needs investment and protection from the whims of those who don't understand it."

The level of support shown toward Smith was considerable, with jeers and applause greeting his more persuasive statements. "Our boats are getting old," he said. "They need new gear, new paint, and repairs to their hulls. We can't invest in keeping them afloat if we're right up against it all year."

The whole atmosphere of the meeting surprised Graham and put him on edge. "Fancies himself as a bit of a local hero, this one," Barnwell muttered to him.

"It's all all right, provided he doesn't suggest anything violent. Then, we'll have a problem." Graham said, not taking his eyes off the scene in front of him.

"We would," Barnwell agreed. "And I'd not be crazy about having to deal with him in front of this lot." Carrying out an arrest while the suspect had the open support of a hundred people wasn't something Graham relished, either.

He quietly hoped the old man would run out of steam, and take it upon himself to sit down.

"But we weren't born yesterday. We understand that fish stocks need time to recover, and that by over-fishing, we're borrowing from tomorrow. Nobody I work with is comfortable with that," Des was loudly proclaiming. The harsh realities of their livelihoods weren't lost on the crowd, who considered the difficulties of an uncertain future as Des pressed on. Graham's mood lifted briefly with this touting of a seemingly moderate position, before Des plunged on again. "But we can't make a living wage with the restrictions they're placing on us, let alone make enough to invest back into our businesses," Des claimed. "The banks aren't interested in helping us out, and the paltry loans and grants the mainland is offering won't even cover the basics. And as for Brexit, pah! What a useless load of buggers those pols are!"

The mention of the European Union brought unpleasant grumbling from the crowd. As everyone knew, Jersey was neither an EU member nor actually part of the UK. Instead, it stood as a third party, with the special status of "overseas territory," and its people hoped that Britain's fraught relationship with Brussels wouldn't damage trade.

"And now the do-gooders have ganged up against us. The green movement tells us we're harvesting the fish unsustainably, pushing them toward extinction, and upsetting the delicate *ecology* of the seas. And the scientists back them up. But you know what? They're busybodies. They'll cook their books and massage their message to make sure we can't make a living. Then, we'll go out of business, our boats will rot in the harbor, and their precious fish can enjoy long and happy lives rollicking about in the sea all while we can't feed our children. It's us against them!" This brought a riot of jeering from the crowd and gained the full focus of Graham's attention. Des sounded angry, skeptical, and put-upon. He was anti-government, anti-EU, anti-conservation, and anti-science. He was proclaiming that the fishermen were being made out to be the bad guys who thought only of the short-term.

"And I haven't even touched on the French!" The mention of their old foe brought cheers and raised fists.

"They're very touched, they are!" someone shouted.

"And they're touching our women!"

There was some scuffling at the back, and Graham pitched onto the balls of his feet like a boxer, alert to the need to intervene. Almost immediately, the fracas subsided away to nothing, and he relaxed again.

"Does that sound something like a motive to you, Constable?" Graham said, in Barnwell's ear.

"Hmm?" Barnwell asked, trying to listen to both Smith and Graham at once.

"He's a bluff old mariner, at the end of his rope, hemmed in on all sides. Tamsin told us that if their research was successful, they could lobby the government to restrict fishing along the migrating sharks pathways. Could that be a reason to want Greg and the Environmental Agency out of the way? That he is a face of 'the enemy?' That his research may disrupt their livelihoods even further?"

Graham watched Barnwell's expression morph from puzzlement to denial, and then to genuine concern. "Des Smith?" Barnwell whispered. "A *murderer*? With respect, sir, pull the other one, it's got bells on."

"Why not? He's angry enough."

"I see what you saying, sir, but...I mean, the idea of it goes beyond 'unlikely,' and well into 'virtually impossible,' if you ask me."

"Hmm, you're probably right." Graham squared his shoulders to lean back against the meeting hall wall. "Still, not bad as theories go. It's worth checking out. If not Des Smith, it could have been someone in this room. All these men want to do is put bread on the table for their families and look forward to retirement in a few years. Right now, they can do neither. Look at them. Any one of them could have followed Somerville out to sea or come across him out on the water. Do they have alibis? We should check."

"What, all of them...?"

"Yes, Constable, all of them."

Barnwell frowned, and looked at Graham out of the corner of his eye. He knew these people. He had lived and worked among them for years. Des Smith was a windbag, no doubt about that, but he was no more a murderer than he, Barnwell, was James Bond. Still, he couldn't dispute the logic behind the DI's wider approach. They would have to check out everyone who owned a boat or came through the harbor in the last few days.

Smith was going for a rousing finale. "So here's what I'm proposing," he said. "We remind ourselves that we're not beholden to anyone. That we're our own little nation state, down here."

Graham made notes. He knew Smith was wrong about Jersey's status, but a true firebrand like him wouldn't let technicalities get in the way of some useful public agitation. His mind cast back to his confrontation with Freddie Solomon a few hours prior. There were similarities between the two men, however different they appeared at face value.

"And we must assert our rights to fish where we like and how we like. We're seafaring folk and we belong at sea, not tied up in the harbor, waiting for some dodgy bureaucrat who has his fingers in the till, or poncing Greenpeace types to tell us when and how we can do our jobs." The crowd was cheering, some on their feet, while the seven-member council sat at the two top tables. They were outwardly impassive but inwardly very worried. A meeting that should have been filled with decorous discussion was turning into the latest salvoes of a bitter war.

Des sat down, exhausted and pale, while the council members restored order. One of them rapped his gavel on the desk in front of him, "Order! Order!"

Barnwell shifted his feet anxiously. "Should we step in, sir?"

"No, stay where you are for the time being. We don't want to stir them up further."

As Barnwell, who was alert to the heightened emotions of the people around him, observed the room, his lips pressed into a thin line, his arms still crossed across his chest, Graham silently tested out his notion that Des Smith, or perhaps one of the other fishermen, was a cold-blooded killer. As a theory, it wasn't perfect, but he had no leads, and the anger he'd seen tonight appeared emblematic of a larger social unease and a disregard for officialdom and lawfulness.

"Looks as though this will end peacefully after all," Barnwell said after a few minutes. Everyone was shuffling out slowly and mostly quietly. "Want me to stay and keep an eye on things?"

His boss was still lost in thought. He was adding up what he knew, shifting the pieces around, trying out new angles and probing some of the less likely investigatory avenues. It was like a collage in his mind, of pictures and ideas, people and places, objects and patterns, connecting and colliding, being dismissed or considered. More than once, when witnessing this silent cogitation, Marcus Tomlinson had requested that Graham puzzle over a case during an MRI, so that his remarkable brain activity could be charted for science. But Graham could already see the salacious headlines: *Inside the Mind of a Top Investigator*, or some such, and had politely declined.

"Sir?" Barnwell tried again, quietly.

"No, lad," the DI finally said, stirring. "We're done here. Go home and get some rest. I'll do the same."

"I think I'll take myself down the pub. It'll be a good way to keep an eye on things too, and keep my ear to the ground. No plans, sir?" He looked innocently at Graham.

The DI looked at his watch, "Not now, no." Out of Barnwell's line of sight, Graham's fists balled briefly, before he flexed them, trying to relax once more.

CHAPTER THIRTEEN

THE CROWD FELL largely silent as Barnwell walked into the pub, but when they saw he was in his civvies, and ostensibly off-duty, the pub's patrons returned to their pints and conversations, a hum and a bustle returning quickly to the pub atmosphere.

Barnwell took a seat at the bar and fired questions at Lewis Hurd whenever the barman wasn't conveying massive plates of food from the kitchen hatch to diners waiting patiently at their tables. He spent a few moments monitoring three French fishermen who were sitting in the corner, talking low, sipping bottles of beer.

"They often come in here?" Barnwell asked Hurd as he returned back from delivering fish and chips times two to a couple at a table near the fireplace.

"They come and go. There's usually a few around, rarely the same ones. They're not the most popular of customers, but I keep an eye on them and they don't cause any real trouble."

"Were there any in here the day Greg Somerville disappeared?"

"There were five of them. Those three," he nodded over to the men in the corner, "and two more."

"When did the other two leave?"

"Oh, they're still here. They were in earlier. They're all stranded. Their boats were damaged in the hurricane. They're working on repairs, if I understood them correctly." Barnwell looked at Hurd, waiting for him to explain.

"My French isn't the best," the barman said with a shrug.

Barnwell turned round, hunching himself over the bar, dangling his bottle of non-alcoholic beer between his thumb and forefinger.

"Tell me about Somerville and his girlfriend."

"They'd been here about four days," the barman recalled of Tamsin and Greg. "They came here the last couple of years as well, chasing whales, or whatever they do."

"Sharks," Barnwell corrected. "How did they seem, together?"

Hurd pulled down a bar towel that was draped over his shoulder and began polishing the wooden surface in front of him and the already-gleaming metal of the eight beer taps that separated him and Barnwell. "How can I put this?" he said, reflecting carefully on what he'd seen. "It's like I used to say about my ex-wife. Can't live with her..."

"Yeah," Barnwell said. "So, a bit of tension between them?"

The barman guffawed. "Tension? I'd say so! Every other time I turned my back, they'd be at each other's throats about some pointless thing or other."

"About their work?"

The barman nodded. "They had this long-running argument that would crop up every now and again. Something about he was the younger one, or the less experienced one, and how his methods weren't as 'sound' as hers. But he reckoned she was overly cautious, old-fashioned, or something. Most of it was Greek to me," he admitted. "Sharks and sensors and what-not. Other than that, they kept themselves to themselves, didn't mingle with the crowd. Just as well, one of those animal rights people has been coming in here. They knew one another. I didn't want any trouble."

"So, they're here together, arguing and carrying on, and then the guy leaves to take his boat out, right?"

"Yeah. And she just sits there for a bit, nursing her pint. Then she shoots off, just leaves her drink half-finished, and disappears out the door," the barman told him, his voice rising at the end of his sentences in surprise. His polishing finished, Lewis tossed the towel back over his shoulder. "Just my two cents, of course. I was listening to them, but also the football on the radio, and seeing to the customers, so I was a bit distracted, like."

"But she definitely left, eh?"

"Oh, yeah. Off like a rocket she was."

"Okay," Barnwell said. "That's useful, thanks." The door to the bar opened and once again the murmur in the room dulled as the pub patrons turned to see who was entering. This time, it was Janice. Jack was with her. He looked bashful as he came through the door, not yet used to the attention Janice garnered through her position, but she smiled broadly and patted one man on the shoulder as she greeted him, inching her way through the crowd to the bar where Barnwell was sitting.

"What can I get you, Janice? Jack?" Barnwell said.

"Two pints of best, please," Janice said. Jack nodded in agreement, his ears pink from the cold air outside.

"Evening, Barry," he said.

"While you're getting that in, I'm just going to pop up to check in on Tamsin. Be back in a sec," Janice said.

Jack and Barnwell chatted as they sipped their drinks, Jack regaling Barnwell with stories of Janice's feisty grandmother and his entry into the Harding family fold.

"Baptism of epic proportions, it was," Jack said, "but I survived." Janice returned from upstairs and joined him at the bar.

"How's she holding up?" Barnwell asked.

Janice made a glum face. "She's not doing so well. I might go back up in a bit, just sit with her so she's not so alone. She's not saying much."

"When she was interviewed, did she say anything about leaving the pub after Somerville?"

"She said she was here all afternoon."

"The boss said she wasn't very helpful."

"No, she didn't say much," Janice agreed.

Barnwell nodded. "Well, even if Tamsin isn't opening up to us yet, the barman was pretty well-informed."

"Oh?" Harding asked.

"Yeah. We've got to speak to the boss. There was an animal activist in here the day Somerville disappeared. He'll want to look into that, and I also have a sneaking feeling he's going to want a more in-depth chat with Ms. Porter after I tell him what I just heard."

CHAPTER FOURTEEN

THE MORNING WIND blew cold off the English Channel, but neither the early hour nor the inclement weather would deter those who had agreed to attend this "extraordinary meeting." They met even before the sun had fully risen, as befit such a rebellious rabble, aboard Des Smith's own fishing boat, the *Queen Sophia*. Des took them a handful of miles out into the Channel and then the six men lit gas camping stoves on the foredeck and produced a large breakfast of eggs, bacon, and richly aromatic smoked fish, the meal protein-laden to prepare them for their tough day ahead.

Des, of course, was the Man of the Moment. His bravura performance at the town hall had spread with remarkable speed, the old mariner's granddaughter already posting an emoji-spattered comment on Smith's Facebook page: *Grandpa! You've gone viral!*

Overnight, recordings of parts of his speech had been shared by campaigners and activists on the mainland, though Des noticed that they avoided those moments where he had slurred his words. He was feeling a little hungover.

For a simple man used to a life of reassuring if challenging routine, this new experience was a little much. When he had left home earlier, he had slammed the door of his fisherman's cottage and had broken out coughing and wheezing as he inhaled. He had leaned on the doorframe, hunched over as he waited for it to pass, wondering what he had got himself into. *Fame, for heaven's sake.* It boggled the mind.

At the harbor, Des met up with five other men aged between thirty and seventy, all of them experienced fishermen or captains, and they'd climbed aboard his boat to motor out to sea, away from prying eyes and ears.

"I just want to say," Len Drake began, "that we're all bloody proud of you for standing up for us as you did last night, Des." Drake was one of the stalwart Gorey captains who'd fished Jersey waters for nigh on fifty years.

"Hear, hear," Flip Mukherjee concurred, raising his steaming mug of tea high in the air. Flip was an Australian of questionable parentage and ethnicity who'd settled on Jersey in his twenties some forty years prior. He owned his own boat and worked it with his son and brother-in-law. An upbeat, friendly character, Flip often found himself the cheerleader among a cohort that tended to despondency. Today was no different.

There was warm applause from the men, and Des received hearty slaps on the back until he begged off for fear of precipitating another coughing fit. The cold sea air was irritating his lungs this morning, as it often did these days.

"Someone needed to stand up," Drake countered. "*Someone* needed to tell these fools that we won't take any more." There were murmurs of agreement.

It was the sound of men at the end of their ropes; a note of sullen and downcast agreement, laced with just a hint of vengeance.

"Well, the world and his mother can see you on YouTube now, apparently," Drake told Des.

"Yeah, but watching the box isn't going to bring about change, now is it?" Des replied.

The men again agreed. Des could see they were tired and angry. The unfairness, the burden of these constant disputes, was weighing heavily on them. Simple men, trying to make a living, were encountering only barriers and prohibitions. Archie "Smokes" Mackenzie, a long-time, grizzled warrior of the seas, flicked a cigarette butt angrily out on to the water.

"It's not as though the industry just sprang up out of the ground, yesterday morning," Drake told them. "We've had *generations* to reach an agreement about stocks and fishing areas."

"But they always say that it's our fault," Phil Whitmore said. Phil, a Yorkshireman, had come down to Jersey three years ago. He'd traveled to the island to get work on the boats after the Kellingley Colliery closed, ending centuries of coal mining in Britain. Used to hard, physical labor, he'd soon made a name for himself among the fishing boat owners and was the first on many of their "Contacts" lists when an extra pair of strong hands was needed. His presence on Des' boat that morning was testimony to the regard in which they held him. "We're 'not being flexible enough', or 'we're simply out for ourselves,' they say."

"'Reluctant to take the long-term view,'" Des added, a phrase with which they were all familiar. "What's the point of even *having* a plan for the long-term? Our short-term prognosis is one word: unemployment."

"Well, I'm not standing around for nuthin.' I'm ready to bring in some extra cash," Matt Crouch told them. Barely thirty, Matt was the youngest man on the boat, though fishing was as much a part of his DNA as any of them. His father had fished the world's oceans, from the Barents Sea to the balmy Chagos Islands, while Matt's grandfather had gone down in a gale not twenty miles from where they now lay at anchor.

"Oh, you got yourself a money-spinner then, eh, Matt?" Des asked him, sheltering his old, darkly polished pipe from the swirling wind as he tried to light it.

"A salvage job, that's the way I see it," he replied. "I've been reading the news, same as you, and nowhere does it say that they've found that bloke's boat."

The other five men thought for a second. "It's gone, though," Drake said. "Hasn't it?"

Matt shrugged, and then, for reasons known only to himself, he adopted the accent of a cowboy from a terrible 1950s Western. "I ain't heard any rumors that it sunk, and I ain't heard no fat lady singin,' so I guess the *Albatross* is still a-bob-bob-bobbin' along around out there somewhere."

Des Smith adjusted to the idea, and the accent, though not without a grimace. "And you're gonna find her, are you?" the old captain asked. Matt looked at him, a little sheepish now. "The boat wasn't found by the Coastguard, even with all their fancy radar, you know?"

"Yeah, but..."

"Neither by a maritime helicopter that has equipment designed *specifically* to find small surface vessels?"

"I know it's a bit of a long shot," Matt admitted, "but I just have a *feeling* about it, you know?"

· They knew. Mariners had been learning to trust their guts since boats were first invented. "Follow your hunch, lad," Des told him eventually, "if you believe in it. But I won't be laying any money on you finding anything. It was only a small'un, and whoever killed that boy wouldn't have risked leaving any trace of it. I reckon the French either took it or sunk it."

He removed his woolen hat and scratched at a thin mat of extremely short, thinning grey hair.

"The French? You think they killed him? Aren't you jumping to conclusions a bit?" Matt Crouch said. He hadn't heard the rumors flying around.

"Well, who else are we to suspect?" Des argued. "He's out there on his own, working to catalog the local wildlife. *We* know that he was counting sharks, but the *French* don't! They're not smart, you know. Have you seen them around town? They're pushing their luck, they are."

"You think they mistook him for a fisheries inspector, or something?"

"They saw him as a *threat*," Des told them. "And they took him out. Or they were sending a *message*."

Matt set aside his empty plate. "That's quite a tall tale, Des," he cautioned. "It's never happened before."

"The French have done everything but *ram* us!" Smith protested. "It's not a big leap from there to a bit of fisticuffs that got out of hand."

"Oh, please," Matt replied. "There's no evidence of any of that. At least," he added, a finger aloft, "not without Greg's boat."

Drake laughed now. "Well, you'd better get out there and track it down, hadn't you?" he said. "Matt Crouch, Marine Detective. You'll make a real name for yourself!"

Des re-started the ship's diesel engine, which gave an unsightly belch of black smoke before catching. As the men, now mostly quiet, finished up their breakfasts, an old idea came up.

"What's wrong with striking for our rights?" Len Drake

posited, but the others saw it for the self-defeating strategy it had so often proved to be.

"The public will figure out pretty quickly that fish from elsewhere is cheaper and more plentiful. They'll buy Spanish mackerel or Icelandic cod instead," said Phil Whitmore. He had plenty of coal mining strike experience behind him and knew it for the risk it was. "We don't have a monopoly, and many of the wholesalers will go elsewhere or do without altogether. Once they find alternatives to fish, or to our fish in particular, they may never come back, and we'll have contracted our market forever."

There was nodding, and the idea of going on strike was put aside as they discussed other forms of complaint and protest. "No point in writing to our MP, either," Des cautioned. "He's more interested in courting big contributors to his election campaign. He's not interested in his constituents at all."

"Useless bugger," Smokes said. The others murmured their agreement.

"Then, how do we get our point across?" asked Matt. A reasonable man, Matt was at a loss. He was as concerned as the others about their livelihoods, especially with a daughter due to arrive in a few weeks. They needed something fresh and new to catch the attention of the big-wigs in London who made all the decisions.

"We'll get ourselves settled in for a protest at the marina," Smith told them. "We don't stop until we have the promise of fair negotiations on quotas." The others were nodding in agreement.

"And an undertaking," Flip Mukhurjee added, "that the Coastguard and Navy let the bloody French know we're protecting our fishing areas." This was greeted with hearty cheers. There was nothing like the prospect of giving the French a slap to lift the spirits of a Jersey fisherman.

"And in the meantime," Matt Crouch said next, "I'll see if I can't get me a handsome little salvage fee. Can I borrow your radar system, Des?"

"Anything you need, son," Des replied. Although he was among the most elderly of the fishermen in the Gorey fleet, Des had never resisted trying new technologies and had a state-of-the-art radar set that would make Matt's search easier. "You go and find that lad's boat, and we'll kick up a fuss at the marina."

Des Smith gunned the engines and steered them back to the harbor with the carefree ease he'd developed over fifty years as a seaman. Sunlight glinted off the choppy waves, the skies were clear. It was going to be a memorable day.

CHAPTER FIFTEEN

G RAHAM WAS SITTING alone in his office with the morning's second pot of tea steaming quietly on a small table in the corner. Its very aroma was invigorating to him, and just as well, he needed all the sustenance and encouragement in the world this morning.

Before him lay the coroner's report on Greg Somerville, and it made for uncomfortable reading. As Tomlinson had indicated earlier, the formal cause of death was blunt instrument trauma. "Environmental experts don't whack themselves over the head with something sharp and heavy," he surmised. "And especially after they've been in a fight."

Graham again played through a number of scenarios in his head. "Who the hell was out there?" Graham murmured out loud. "And did they happen upon him, or set out deliberately to find him? And why?"

Only when Graham spotted Barnwell lurking at his open office door did his imagination return from the cold tracts of the English Channel and engage once more with the present. "Morning, Barnwell."

"Morning, sir," the burly constable replied. The big man cut quite a different figure to the one that first greeted Graham on his arrival in Gorey. Back then, Barnwell had been the butt of jokes, a corpulent and patently unfit officer, occasionally turning up for duty suffering the consequences of a previous night's hard drinking. His likely prospects amounted to finding himself alternately and reluctantly pounding the beat and manning the front desk throughout an unspectacular career. But now, Barnwell stood tall, the image of a confident and well-prepared investigator. He'd lost weight – perhaps forty pounds altogether – and having taken up swimming and boxing in recent months, looked much more agile on his feet and alert around the eyes. It was a remarkable transformation, one in which Graham felt a small amount of pride, though the achievement was Barnwell's alone.

Barnwell stood in the doorway to Graham's office, looking hesitant and a little apologetic.

"What's up, Constable?" Graham asked.

"Janice and Roach are out interviewing fishermen as you requested, sir."

"Good, good," Graham said. He waited. "And...?"

"It's line one, sir," the constable replied. "I'm afraid it's Mrs. Taylor again."

Graham dropped the pen he'd been twirling between his fingers. "Evil spirits, is it?" he asked.

Barnwell shrugged. "She's adamant, sir." He was often the bearer of unwelcome news, and though Mrs. Taylor presented no more than a minor irritant, it did bother Barnwell that he was so frequently a carrier of such tidings. Just once, he'd like to appear at Graham's office door and announce that Janice had collared someone, or that Roach had picked up a burglar wanted in Paris but who was hiding out on the island. Maybe even a fugitive drug lord or a noto-rious human trafficker. But mostly, Barnwell's job was seem-ingly to add more complication to David Graham's professional life.

"Bloody hell," the DI moaned. "All right, put her through. But if I'm not off the phone in four minutes flat, knock on my door with something urgent, all right?"

Barnwell blinked. "Urgent, sir?"

Graham reached for the receiver and sighed again. "Use your imagination, Constable. Anything will do. Just give me the nod, okay?" Then, with a lighter tone that was just this side of forced, he said into the phone, "Good morning, Mrs. Taylor. What can Gorey Constabulary do for you this..."

Barnwell returned to the reception desk and watched Graham through his office doorway as the Detective Inspector listened to Mrs. Taylor's latest story. It was quite an entertaining display. The DI would spark into life at the least sign of something interesting, or plunge into sallow disappointment at the receipt of bad news. Barn-well knew at once when Mrs. Taylor said something inter-esting, and then moments later, he saw that she'd somehow ruined things and that the DI was in danger of losing his patience. Barnwell kept his eye on the wall clock behind Graham's desk, ready to intervene at the four-minute mark.

"I know how this sounds," Marjorie Taylor admitted to Graham on the other end of the phone, "I know you'll think I've gone loopy, yammering on about spirits and such."

Graham knew that this rare, and to him, unexpected example of Mrs. Taylor's enthusiasm for the paranormal had to be handled with care. "In this job," Graham explained mildly, careful that his tone couldn't be construed as dismissive, "I have to reach for scientific explanations, but

I also have to listen to people when they claim to have evidence."

This encouraged Mrs. Taylor sufficiently that Graham couldn't get a word in edgewise for ninety seconds. "It's just like my sister said," she related with gusto. "A huge storm, lots of damage, and then the *strangest* goings-on in the days after. People disappearing. Things moving around in the kitchen. And you know how proud I am of my kitchen, Detective Inspector."

"I do, indeed, Mrs. Taylor," Graham demurred, "I've used the phrase 'as clean as Mrs. Taylor's kitchen floor' more than once when dismissing suspects."

"Have you?"

There was a pause and Graham imagined Mrs. Taylor puffing with a little self-conscious pride at being mentioned in a positive light with respect to a criminal investigation, however tenuous the connection.

"Well, it's not clean today!" Mrs. Taylor complained. "There are cans of tomatoes rolling around, half my fruit salad is missing, some of my pots and pans are definitely *not* where I left them, and I found my *bain marie* smashed to pieces when I came down this morning."

"So, Mrs. Taylor," he said. "You're there, and you know what you see. Help me understand what *you* think happened."

Her reply was brief. "There are bad spirits abroad," she said. "Think what you like, David." It was the very first time she'd used his name, in all the long months since he'd originally appeared, suitcase in hand, at the reception desk of the White House Inn. "But I know it."

Barnwell knocked loudly on Graham's door, hoping that Mrs. Taylor might hear at the other end of the phone. He glanced up at the clock. "Sorry to disturb, sir."

"No problem, Constable," Graham said. Then, into the receiver, "I'm sorry, Mrs. Taylor, but Constable Barnwell needs me." He then only partly covered the receiver with his hand, and asked Barnwell, "Problem, Constable?"

"The castle's on fire, sir."

"Right, sorry, Mrs. Taylor, we've got to go. Castle's on fire." He looked at Barnwell, pursing his lips. He lifted his free palm upward in a "what the hell?" gesture.

"David?" Mrs. Taylor said before he hung up. "David, please listen. I know what this is." He'd never heard her sound more deadly serious. "And I know the threat we're all facing. It won't stop, ever. Not until we deal with this other world..." she paused, seeming to search for the right word, "*entity*." She bid him a good day and hung up.

Graham blinked a few times after replacing the receiver. "Well."

"Well?" Barnwell asked. "Has Mrs. Taylor gone to the zoo?"

Graham shook his head. "Not quite yet, lad. But maybe soon. And let's hope she doesn't check the news for the status of some fiery Armageddon at the castle on her way."

Barnwell grinned at his boss. "Sorry, sir. It was the first thing that came to mind." He noted the report on Graham's desk. "I was in the pub last night, and the barman told me that Tamsin Porter didn't remain there all afternoon the day Somerville went missing like she said."

Graham sat back abruptly in his chair. "Did she now? Well, well, well." He looked out of the window, twirling his pen some more.

After a minute of silence, Barnwell ventured, "What do you make of Ms. Porter now, sir?"

"I'm thinking that things are never as simple as they

should be," Graham said. "If lying were impossible, I'd be able to retire and hand things over to a trainee constable."

"Perish the thought, sir. None of us would have jobs."

"Hmm, true. I'm wondering what caused her to hide that piece of information from us. What do you think, Barnwell?"

"She's a smart, educated woman, sir, rather stroppy and unhappy, but that's not surprising under the circumstances. She wouldn't be the first to expose a dark side when a relationship is breaking down."

"But what else might we observe about her, Constable? What informed inference can we deduce from her behavior?" Graham pressed.

Barnwell reflected for a moment. Graham's invitations to think more deeply about a question were never his way of simply killing time or even a surefire way of being thorough; there was always *an intent* to these questions. He began to feel a little put on the spot. He looked around and rubbed his palms together. "How's that different from plain, old *guesswork,* sir?" "Informed inference" was becoming one of Graham's go-to expressions, but Barnwell wasn't sure that it wasn't some kind of investigative double-speak.

Graham looked shocked, as though Barnwell had proposed dropping their investigation and was heading out to the pub. "I never *guess*, Constable," Graham reminded him. "You know that. I make informed summations from the information that we gather."

"And what have we gathered?" Barnwell asked, keen to move Graham's focus off of him. For a missing person's case, they had vanishingly little to go on.

"Somerville was a scientist. And, like most people, scientists have enemies," Graham said. "That if he'd been successful in getting additional protection for these sharks,

that would have impinged upon fishing areas already allo-
cated to the Jersey fleet. We also know that his relationship
was breaking down and that his girlfriend has lied to us
about her whereabouts on the afternoon he disappeared."

"And the barman also told me there is an animal activist
in town. He knew the couple and not in a friendly kind of
way, neither," Barnwell added.

"Is that so? Well, looks like we've gathered that our
scientist had rather *a lot* of enemies, wouldn't you say? You
should go down the pub more often, Constable. That's some
good investigative work you've done there."

"You don't really think the fishermen had anything to
do with this, do you?"

Graham shrugged. "My concern there is that someone
may have gone out to confront Greg, or perhaps they were
already at sea when they saw him, and then when he'd been
killed – either by accident or design – someone started a
rumor to link his death with the French as a form of cover-
up. From what I saw last night at the town hall, the men are
so up in arms, they'd blame the French for anything that
was even remotely plausible, and perhaps protect their own
in the process. We could be heading for an international
incident."

Barnwell was shaking his head. "I don't believe it, sir.
The men just aren't like that. They are a family, a
constantly warring family perhaps, but a family nonetheless. And while Greg Somerville wasn't a fisherman, and
you could argue that his research worked against the fishermen's interests, they all care about the marine life in their
own way. Really, Somerville had more in common with the
fishermen than we do."

"Maybe, maybe. But remember it would only take one
rogue fisherman to decide to take someone out. It's not

perfect as theories go, certainly. And the idea that it was Des Smith borders on the far-fetched, but it is a workable hypothesis. Hopefully, the interviews that Harding and Roach are doing will clarify things. In the meantime, find this activist and check his alibi. Report back to me when you've done that, okay?" Graham sat forward in his chair and rapped his desk with the end of his pen. "All right, back to work, eh? No rest for the wicked."

"Yes sir!"

Outside, the phone rang, and Barnwell returned to the reception desk, leaving Graham with the strange and unwelcome fallout from Mrs. Taylor's ghost story and a list of unanswered questions relating to the Somerville murder.

"A dead marine biologist. An untruthful girlfriend. A possible saboteur. Angry fishermen. Gorey up in arms," he muttered to himself. "And now some idiot's trashing Mrs. Taylor's kitchen at night, apparently without stealing anything, except for a bit of fruit salad." He made notes as he always did, in a mixture of detailed text and rather more artistic "mind-maps," little sketches that summarized his thoughts pictographically. He drew a dark, brooding storm cloud with forks of lightning stretching out to connect the different elements: *"Fishermen," "The French," "Sharks," "Greg Somerville," "Girlfriend," "Animal Rights,"* and on, until he'd laid out the entire confusing case. Then, he connected the colorful whole with another strand, a broken line: *"Poltergeist at the White House Inn?"*

Outside his office, the doors to the station burst open, and in blew Sergeant Roach encased head to foot in wet weather gear. He stood in reception for a moment, the rain dripping off the end of his jacket, making puddles on the floor as he caught his breath.

"Is it raining, Jim?" Barnwell asked him.

"What do you think, smartarse?" Roach replied. "I'm ready for this weather to be over."

"So how did you get on?" Roach pushed the hood of his jacket off his head. Drops of rain ran down his face.

"I got something. I followed up with the Harbormaster, about what you said about Tamsin Porter," he said, unzipping his jacket and pulling out his notebook from his uniform pocket. He flipped it open and wiped a drop of rain from the end of his nose with the back of his hand.

"Tamsin Porter in the Billy Alley, left the harbor at 12:33 PM; returned 12:57 PM," he read.

Barnwell consulted the Somerville case file. "That's just ten minutes after Somerville went out. She followed him."

"Yep," Roach said, now stepping out of his big, wide waterproofs. "That's what I reckon, too."

"Well, you'd better go tell the guv'nor."

CHAPTER SIXTEEN

F REDDIE SAT NEXT to three piles of books, newspapers, and periodicals, writing with feverish intensity on a yellow legal pad. His work had spread until it dominated one of the main reading tables in the center of the library, but the other patrons didn't seem to mind. Freddie had become a household name in Gorey, and he had far more avid readers than detractors. He filled another page with shorthand, making extensive notes on a storm that had wiped out several of the fishing fleets over a hundred years before.

"Are you finding everything you need?" Laura asked as she passed by his desk on the first of her morning patrols.

Freddie glanced up at her, pleased that the librarian was taking an interest in his work. Enthusiasts of the *Gorey Gossip* were instant friends to Freddie, and all the more quickly if they happened to be gorgeous. "Oh, yes," he said, with a charming smile. "Fascinating story. 'The Christmas Storm of nineteen-eleven.' It's a tale well worth telling again, in our present context."

Laura took a look at the encyclopedias and maritime

histories that Freddie had spread across the broad, wooden desk. "Amazing to think," she said quietly, so as not to disturb two elderly readers who were relaxing in armchairs and engrossed in the day's *Racing Post* within earshot of them, "that there isn't a single person left on Jersey who was alive back then."

Freddie's network of sources meant that the island's seniors were very much his bailiwick. "Old Mrs. Parkinson will be a hundred and one in the spring," he said, "but no, I guess she'd need to be at least a hundred and ten to remember that storm."

"So, you're writing about historical events relating to storms off Gorey?" Laura asked. Although she didn't care to read Freddie's blog, like everyone else, perhaps with the exception of the local constabulary, she found him rather charming on the surface. She also knew that some of his methods were unsavory, and that he had come under David's scrutiny for releasing information before the police were ready. On one occasion, he'd mentioned the unfortunate necessity of giving Solomon a "thorough dressing-down." For reasons Laura couldn't quite pin down, this "bad boy" image merely compounded the young writer's appeal, certainly among the locals who were apt to view him as a minor celebrity.

"I'm working to draw parallels between them and the storm we just had," Solomon explained. "I had a local tip about strange happenings in these parts following major storms."

This, too, rang a bell with Laura. Hadn't David mentioned something about Mrs. Taylor losing the plot and seeing ghosts or some such? "Do you think there's anything to it?" she asked, genuinely interested.

Freddie pulled out the chair next to him and motioned

for her to sit before showing her a selection of clippings, articles, and yellowed newspapers dating back well over a century. "It seems to be a repeating pattern," Freddie told her. "A gale blows up and causes loss of life and damage, and within the few days immediately after, there's always an *incident* of some sort."

Laura frowned and skimmed two of the articles, impressing Freddie, who was no slouch at speed reading himself. "Well, it's all very interesting, but you know what they say about *correlation* and *causation*."

"Oh, yes," Freddie replied, "and the Gorey police seem to agree with you. But," he said, suddenly reflective, "when investigating a case, I think it's prudent to examine *all* the angles, don't you?"

"Sounds sensible," Laura said, careful to speak in a neutral tone.

Freddie saw that his subtle dig at the local police had been met with pursed lips, but no impassioned defense. In Freddie's view, that was a very good sign.

Laura was different, he'd already decided. There was a certain calm competence about her, and an unstinting enthusiasm for helping others learn. These were her less obvious traits. Most people, especially men, would be instantly taken with Laura's good looks. In his mind, Freddie compared her to a young Grace Kelly or blond Audrey Hepburn; slender, tall, seemingly unintimidating, but possessed of considerable inner strength. And she was unfailingly polite, he noted too, something he found reassuringly wholesome.

"Let me know if you need help finding anything else," Laura said, standing up. She moved on to check in with a regular who was trying to find something in the health section. Once she had answered his questions and sent him to the right shelf, she returned to the main desk and continued with the day's more mundane work – labeling new items and entering their details into the computer. As she typed, she found her mind, and then eventually her eyes, drawn back to Freddie as he read and wrote in that effervescent way of his.

Laura compared him to David. Freddie was younger, smaller, slighter, and more colorful. He was also morally flexible and opportunistic, two labels that could never be applied to Graham. But Freddie was more "available."

Laura was no more beholden to the Inspector than he was to her, and he'd already made it crystal clear that his responsibilities as a police officer handily trumped his personal life. Laura guessed that went for *her* personal life too, if hers were connected to his. There had been a handful of evenings that one might call dates, but they'd only managed to reach the end of two of them, the others being curtailed for one reason or another. Further arrangements had been canceled or rescheduled, often at the shortest possible notice. But still, she respected him for his professionalism, commitment, steadiness, intelligence, and his moral code.

Was it selfish then, Laura wondered, that she wanted more from him? Was she being childish if a small ripple of resentment toward his work, his colleagues, the countless, endless hours, the dangers he sometimes faced, ran through her? Laura sighed and snapped out of her reverie. She found Freddie Solomon standing on the other side of the issue desk, watching her intently. "Oh, sorry," she said, laughing. "I was miles away. What can I do for you?"

Freddie was feeling bold and decided that he'd strike while the iron was hot. Or, if not actually *hot*, then encouragingly warm. "I did wonder whether you might be a bit of a daydreamer," he said quietly, well out of earshot of the other patrons. "Was it anything good?" There was a conspiratorial glint in his eye, as if encouraging Laura to divulge that which she should not.

"Oh, it was nothing," she said, shutting down Freddie's inquiry as gently as she could. "Just got a bit distracted for a moment. You need anything?"

Freddie summoned all of his courage. Despite his flamboyant persona, he often found himself tongue-tied around beautiful women, and Laura was certainly the most striking he'd seen in Gorey for a long while. "I, er, wondered," he began, "if I could tempt you to join me for coffee one morning. When you're not working, that is." His words sounded confident. Inwardly, he braced himself for what he was certain would be a polite refusal.

But he could see that she was torn. Laura hesitated and when the anticipated immediate refusal didn't occur, Freddie allowed himself to have just a little hope.

"I'm sorry," Laura responded eventually. "I'm seeing someone." *Was that the right phrase?* A noisy melée began in her mind, a confused battle between her desire for a relationship with David Graham and the reality of only the modest commitment to her that he seemed able to make.

Freddie's face fell, but he hid the bulk of his disappointment. "I wasn't aware, I'm sorry," he said. "Anyone I know?"

Laura chuckled. "In a manner of speaking. I understand you've already had a cordial chat with Detective Inspector Graham."

Freddie's eyes closed, and he burst out laughing. "Oh, my," was all he said at first. But then he couldn't resist. "A fine detective," he announced. "Wedded to his job and his rule book."

Much was implied in those few words. To her, it was a

reminder that a senior police investigator was unsuitable relationship material; that he'd be forever distracted by cases and administrative problems, would lack the time to make a go of it with her, and she'd not receive the attention she deserved. There was also a not-so veiled insult in Freddie's tone, and it sparked a flash of angry defensiveness that Laura quickly tamped down.

"Very fine, indeed," Laura confirmed. "A remarkable mind. Anyway," she said breezily, "let me know if you need help finding anything else."

Freddie returned to his table and began to pack up his research. He felt awkward, but at the same time, he'd learned a new piece of gossip, news that might at some point come in very useful, indeed.

CHAPTER SEVENTEEN

"**M**S. PORTER," GRAHAM said as he and Harding began another interview with Tamsin. "I hope you don't mind meeting in these more informal surroundings." The section of the pub nearest the back door was almost empty and was as good a place to talk as any.

"It's fine," Tamsin said. Graham could see that she'd barely slept, and that her demeanor and appearance were those of someone who was carrying an immense emotional weight. "I want to help." She seemed a little more cooperative than she had the previous day.

Once more, Graham retraced Greg's steps on the morning of his disappearance, asking for Tamsin's confirmation at each stage. "And there had been a kind of disagreement between you," Graham said. It wasn't really a question, but Tamsin nodded. "Was he angry when he left?"

She thought back, and the pain of recollection showed in her face. "It was bitter, between us, sometimes," she admitted. "I said some things, he said some things. You know how it is."

Graham flipped a page in his notebook. "I think I do," he said. "But something I also now know is that *you* left Gorey Harbor during the early afternoon. A second Environmental Agency launch was seen heading out in the direction of the buoys with you in it." He waited for Tamsin to signal that she'd forgotten this detail, though he silently hoped she might simply collapse into a full confession even if he did think it unlikely.

Instead, her response was quite strange. She blinked repeatedly as though struggling to come to terms with something, but then blurted out, "I should have told you earlier."

Harding's fingers were alive on her iPad, but Graham studied the young woman very closely as she spoke. "I went out in my launch to catch up with Greg. I wanted to put things right, to help him with the equipment, record the data."

Harding asked the most obvious question before Graham could even prompt her. "Why didn't you mention this earlier?"

Tamsin's reply was a shrug that begged for forgiveness in these days of grief. "Have you ever lost anyone?" she asked Harding. And then she turned to Graham, her eyes inquiring and pleading, but he didn't respond. *Not now, not here, not to you, and certainly not in front of Harding.*

"The bottom fell out of my world. You can't imagine. Maybe I forgot some details, my mind was a mess," Tamsin said.

"Did you find him?" Harding asked next.

"No. I abandoned the idea almost immediately. He wasn't where I expected. Maybe he got a fault signal from a buoy further out and headed for that straight away, I don't know. He could have been anywhere. I quickly gave it up as a bad job and turned back."

"So, you didn't encounter his boat, and you saw no sign of him?"

"That's right. I guess I sat alone on the water for a few minutes looking around, and when I couldn't see him, I headed back to the pub to wait for him to return."

"You didn't radio him to find out where he was?"

Tamsin shrugged. "No, I wasn't sure he would welcome my presence, and I suppose I didn't want confirmation of that. It seemed easier just to turn around. It was another four or five hours before I declared him overdue and all of this began." Tamsin's grip on her emotions was still slender, and she took a moment to collect herself before suddenly sitting bolt upright. "We had problems with the engine on the launch, two days before the storm. Greg thought the wrong type of fuel was in the tank. We'd never make that type of mistake, so we thought that someone was actively sabotaging us. Maybe his death has something to do with that?" Her eyes narrowed. "Have you accounted for all the fishermen?"

"Well," Graham said, "that's difficult. There are many, but we are working through them—"

Tamsin stood. "I'm going down there right now. To the marina." She was fired up, angry, and resolute.

"Wait!" Harding cried, but Tamsin roughly pulled open the bar door and was gone.

Janice turned to Graham who was still sitting in his chair, his elbow on the arm as he calmly watched Tamsin through the window. "Well, we lost control of that one, sir."

"We know where she's going. She won't get far." He pushed himself out of his seat, "But let's get after her."

Tamsin had run down the sloping path to the harbor at speed. She would reach it in no time.

"Are we going to have trouble?" Harding wondered to Graham. "The men are not going to like her throwing accusations around."

"True," Graham said, breathing steadily as they jogged down the slope. "But I'm keen to see their reaction, all the same."

Down at the harbor, Smith, Drake, Mukherjee, and Mackenzie were carrying out their plan to stage a protest. They and a dozen others were holding signs which read, "*Honk if you respect Jersey's fishermen!*" and, "*More Mussels, Less Brussels.*"

Unsurprisingly, Tamsin found them easily enough.

"I want to speak to you," she said bullishly, approaching Des Smith. "I want some answers."

Harding and Graham caught up with her. "Are you suggesting that these men have something to do with Greg's disappearance?" Janice asked.

"Yeah," Tamsin blurted again. "One of you guys interfered with Greg's boat. I know it. You never liked having us around from the start."

Des actually dropped his pipe. "Say that again, young lady." He sounded equal parts of confused and combative.

"You don't want 'government types' around down here," she asserted. "You'd do anything to get us off your backs, to get us out of your fishing lanes. One of you probably killed him!"

Graham and Harding were treated to the noisy spectacle of Des Smith in one of his favorite guises: angry and aggrieved. "What? You come down here, spouting all kinds of nonsense, accusing decent, hard-working men of *murder*, for heaven's sake!" He turned to Graham. "Can't you do something? Isn't this, I don't know, libel or slander, or something?"

Graham took Tamsin gingerly by the arm. "I couldn't say," he admitted, "but I do know Ms. Porter is very upset."

"You're damn right, I'm upset!" she shrieked, wrenching her arm from Graham. "No one is looking in the right place! You're all wasting your time!"

"Come with me, Tamsin," Janice said quietly. She gazed directly at the other woman signaling her concern, and some of the fire in Tamsin's eyes went out.

Harding walked her away from the group. "I know you're upset, and we'll ask them some questions, Tamsin, but you really can't go around accusing people like that." Tamsin very gradually settled down, muttering to herself and to Harding, until the sergeant was able to escort her back to the pub.

Another half-hour of questions achieved nothing.

"As I've already said, we had an argument. I went out to look for him. I returned quickly, having not sighted him, and I waited in our room at the pub until I called him in missing. The end." Tamsin spread her hands, "That's all there is to it. Now, if you don't mind, I would appreciate you leaving me alone to face another day of trying to piece my life together. Greg's parents are arriving from Norfolk later today. They were enjoying a quiet retirement until this happened. Instead, somehow, we'll be putting together funeral arrangements and packing up Greg's belongings."

The incredible strain showed in her every facial expression and movement. As they left, Harding gave her a pitying glance, but she knew there was little to be done.

"Wow," the sergeant noted when Tamsin had left. "I'm not sure what to think. Part of me is incredibly sympathetic, but really? She went out in her boat? And the boat had been sabotaged? And she's only telling us this now?"

Graham wore that intense frown – not joyless, but determined – which betrayed the avid workings of a keen mind. "People under stress do forget things," he allowed, "but those are huge omissions to make at a time like this."

"Is she still a suspect, sir?" Harding asked. Despite her exasperation with Tamsin's lack of transparency, her own quiet hope was that the woman could be eliminated from their inquiries and allowed to grieve in peace.

"I'd say she's our *number one* suspect, Sergeant. She had a form of motive, and the opportunity while they were alone at sea together."

"And the method?" Harding pressed, applying Graham's own rubric. It was fun to extemporize, but she knew all too well that guesswork was unscientific.

"Pretty well any boat afloat in the world today has a tool that could be repurposed as a murder weapon...We need to search her launch, just in case it was her and she was silly enough to leave the evidence behind."

Tamsin's launch was tied up next to other vessels of its type – essentially large dinghies with a single, powerful, outboard motor. It only took seconds of searching to conclude there was absolutely nothing out of the ordinary. "I mean, it's too much to ask for her to put a sign up saying, 'Murder weapon here – please dust for prints,' but there's just no evidence of anything," Janice commented.

There were no obvious footprints, no signs of a struggle, no damage to the vessel. Literally nothing Graham could associate with Greg Somerville's death.

CHAPTER EIGHTEEN

THE SMALL GATHERING at the harbor quickly developed into a major protest, complete with banners and loudhailers. Representatives from the island's tiny media outlets were in attendance, and it was likely that the demonstration would find itself deserving of a slot on the evening TV news. Smith was enthused and passionate, arguing the fishermen's case with passers-by, shouting in response to the five Frenchmen who jeered as they walked along the promenade, delivering vigorous clap backs, and accompanied by appropriate hand gestures. He even gave an interview to that ubiquitous presence in times of trouble, Freddie Solomon.

But by three o'clock, the character of the noisy protest had changed. After arriving back onshore and collecting Des Smith's radar, Matt Crouch had headed straight back out to sea in search of Greg Somerville's boat. Now, six hours later, word was spreading that Crouch could not be reached. "We've tried his radio every five minutes for the last two hours," Drake explained when asked for news of the younger fisherman. "If his radio fails, he's got the satellite back-up, but he's not responding on that, either."

The crowd had began to worry, and by four o'clock, with a half-dozen pairs of binoculars scanning the horizon, and still no sign that Matt was heading back to harbor for the night, Smith put a call in to the Coastguard. When their muted response was unsatisfactory, Smith called the Constabulary. Minutes later, Graham and Barnwell showed up, anxious for news.

"It's Matt Crouch. He went looking for Greg Somerville's boat," Smith explained to them. He was a lot more comfortable talking to the familiar Barnwell than his rather aloof boss, but Graham listened well and asked searching questions.

"Why did he head out alone? How unusual is it for him to be this overdue?" Graham quickly learned that he knew even less about the affairs of the sea than he'd hoped.

"We're often alone," Drake told him. "If we're hauling fish, then there's maybe two or three of us, but Matt just went out for a quick look at a patch of water. No need for other hands. He might have stayed out for a bit, but it's his not returning our calls that's worrying us. First rule of the sea: keep in touch."

"I don't mean to place any blame, I'm simply trying to understand," the DI explained gently. "But what did he hope to find that a thorough Coastguard search had not? They've got all the fanciest electronics equipment."

This opened the floodgates for a veritable torrent of complaint about the Coastguard being under-funded, under-staffed, and unable to retain competent crew. "It's practically a charity. We have to help them out all the time, as do the RNLI," Smith explained. "It's not like the Royal

Navy, or the US Coast Guard they have in America. They're part of the military over there. Armed and everything, they are." His point was a little disingenuous. Her Majesty's Coastguard was primarily a search and rescue service, not tasked with the responsibilities of other nation's Coastguard units, and local fishing boats, leisure craft, and lifeboats supplemented the service when time was of the essence, rescue at sea operations nearly always being a race against time. Even civilian spotter planes and French helicopters were called on to help if necessary. "And that new chap, the one in charge at St. Helier..." Des continued to rant.

Barnwell's initial findings, that Brian Ecclestone was prickly and awkward to deal with, had become a general consensus. "He's mean with his resources," Smith complained. "Refuses requests – left, right, and center – and hasn't the foggiest about what our fishing fleet has to deal with. He wouldn't even send the 'Guard out to look for Matt without your say so."

"So when did Matt Crouch leave the harbor?" Graham interjected quickly when Des paused to draw breath.

"It's a miracle we find any bloody fish at all with what we have to deal with," Smith continued, ignoring him. "Ten-ish I'd say," he ended, answering Graham's question so off-handedly that the DI nearly missed it.

Des' anger re-ignited the protest and there were long minutes of slogan-chanting and a chorus of honking motorists.

Graham pulled Smith away from the crowd. He wasn't certain that the old man wasn't discreetly hitting the bottle in between each heartfelt airing of grievances. "We've put a Search-And-Rescue request in," Graham said.

"Hmph, good luck. I bet he cites all kinds of reasons why Matt's fine. He knows that if he delays long enough, we'll go look for him ourselves."

With Des away from the group, Barnwell chatted to the other fishermen, all of whom repeated the same story of Matt's plans and his troubling failure to return to harbor. At his boss' shoulder, and as Des returned to his group, he whispered, "What do you think, sir? Should we be worried? Two men disappearing out at sea in strange circumstances within days of one another is a bit suspect."

"I think it's too soon to say, although I imagine Mrs. Taylor would have a different view on the matter."

"The men here certainly do, sir. They keep mentioning the French, the ones that hang around town?"

"I think, Constable, that those who come ashore are troublemakers, baiting the locals, stirring things up, but I don't think there's anything more there. They're just a convenient bogeyman for Smith and his ilk. What else have you got?"

"Ecclestone's coming in for some real stick, sir, but he's got a SAR helicopter on the way."

"Excellent, lad," the DI told Barnwell. "Hopefully, we'll get Matt home before dark and this will all be forgotten." The weather forecast for the night was badly unsettled, with squally showers and high winds.

"I'll be heading out with them, sir," Barnwell added. "They like to have someone from the Constabulary join them if there's a sense of anything crime-related."

Graham looked puzzled. "But... they fly off the pad at St. Helier."

"They do, sir," Barnwell confirmed.

"And I can't help noticing that you're not *in* St. Helier,

Constable." Graham turned away from the fishermen who continued to blow off steam at any passer-by with enough time to listen.

Barnwell's answer was to glance skyward from where a familiar clattering sound was growing louder. The helicopter, a big, broad, functional design with an immensely powerful main engine rotating its spinning blades, eased over the top of the castle and slowed to a noisy hover over the beach.

"Low tide, sir," Barnwell yelled over the din. "Not a bad spot to land. They said they couldn't resist dropping in and offering me a lift."

The chopper pilot lowered his machine down to the beach while Graham ushered the fishermen to a safer distance. None were unimpressed by the sight of this flying monster descending among them. Des Smith, frustrated at this momentary disturbance to their protests, was simultaneously relieved that the "big guns" were going out in search of Matt. He was uncharacteristically silent. The chopper's wheels touched down softly on the yielding sand, and Barnwell gave his boss a thumbs up before dashing, hand on his head, under the wash of the spinning rotor. A crewman opened the sliding door and ushered Barnwell in. Graham could see him getting strapped in even as the pilot urged the engines above idle. Moments later, the rotors caught the chilly evening air, and the helicopter rose steadily once more into a slate-gray sky.

To Graham, it was like watching a giant bathtub sprout wings, take off, and somehow head out to sea. *Not a bad way to get to work.* Part of him envied Barnwell, but there was much work to do here on shore. Amid the noisy wash of the helicopter's departure, the honking of supportive drivers, and the full-throated chanting of the angered fishermen, Graham entirely failed to notice three new texts from Laura.

CHAPTER NINETEEN

J ANICE KNOCKED ON the door of the neat, modern, terraced house and looked up and down the street. Either side of it was lined with rows of identical homes. A couple of young boys aged around seven were playing on their bikes while close by two young girls were kneeling on the path drawing pink and blue flowers with sticks of chalk. A couple of cones, one with a red flag poking out of it, had been put out to act as a warning to drivers who were apt to travel too fast down this straight, narrow road.

The door opened and Janice turned to face the heavily pregnant young woman who stood in front of her. "Mrs. Crouch? Cheryl? I'm here from the local constab—"

"Is there any word?" The woman's short, brown hair flopped over her eyes. She pushed it behind her ear. She looked at Janice, her pupils bright with fear.

"No, no word, Mrs. Crouch. May I come in?"

"Yes, of course. Please go through to the kitchen. We're in there," the woman said indicating toward a door at the end of the hall. She stood back and flattened herself against the wall, the narrow hallway made even more so by the advanced state of her pregnancy.

"Please, after you," Janice said.

Janice followed Cheryl Crouch into the small, boxy kitchen where, leaning back against the cabinets was a man cradling a mug of tea in his folded arms. He met Janice's eye reluctantly and rubbed his cheekbone. Janice noticed a bruise forming there. Cheryl Crouch came over to him and put her hand on his arm.

"This is Phil. He's a friend of Matt's. He's come over to sit with me until...until..." The woman's voice broke.

"Come on, Cheryl, love," the man said. He put an arm around her.

"Here," Janice pulled out a chair from the kitchen table and Cheryl Crouch allowed herself to be passed between the pair. She levered herself heavily down onto the seat, covered her cheeks with the palms of her hands and closed her eyes.

Janice sat down next to her. "I just wanted to ask you, Cheryl, about Matt's movements. When did you last see him?" Cheryl lowered her hands from her face, and they flittered to a pendant that lay around her neck. She slid it back and forth on its cord.

"He left early this morning, to go on Des Smith's boat. Phil went too."

Phil nodded. "That's right. We all went out for a bit of a chat."

Cheryl continued, "When he came back, he popped in to say he was going out to look for that scientist's boat. I wasn't too keen because it's still a bit rough after the storm, but he didn't pay any attention."

"And how did he seem?"

"Seem?" Cheryl looked up at Janice, frowning.

"Yes, in himself," Janice said, gently. She glanced up at Phil, then back at Cheryl.

"F-fine. Normal." Cheryl's voice got stronger. She sat up a little straighter and stopped playing with the green pendant. "What do you think, Phil? Did he seem okay to you?"

Phil shrugged. "Seemed so, seemed perfectly normal. He wanted to go looking for the boat. He'd have made a bit of money if he'd have found it."

Janice knew that the boat would have been impounded as evidence the moment it turned up, but said nothing.

"So he came back in after your meeting on Des' boat, popped in here, then straight out again? And you haven't heard from him since?"

"That's right. It's been hours now. I sent him a text asking him to tell me when he was leaving the Harbor. I always like him to do that, but he didn't reply." Cheryl pulled her phone over to her from where it sat on the table, "That was at 10:09 this morning."

"That's 'bout right," Phil said. "We were back here at eight-thirty, nine. He would've popped back here, then gone to the boat, tidied her up a bit, and off he'd have gone."

"Hmm, okay." Janice wrote this all down on her iPad and logged off. "We've got the Coastguard helicopter out looking for him, Cheryl, and some of his mates have gone out in their boats too. We're doing everything we can to find him," she said. The temptation was to share some platitude, to promise Cheryl that her husband would come home very soon, safe and sound, but her words would be meaningless, and she knew that the woman in front of her knew they would be, too.

Instead, Janice patted Cheryl's hand and gave her a sympathetic smile. "We're doing our best for him, okay?"

Cheryl, her face crumpling, looked down into her lap as she rubbed her swollen belly. Janice stood and pressed her hand to the pregnant woman's shoulder as she passed. "I'll see myself out," she said to Phil.

As Janice opened the front door to the fading light of the day, she heard Phil Whitmore come up behind her.

"She's very upset," he said.

"That's understandable, of course." Janice looked at the tall, handsome man who she estimated was a few years older than his friend. "Tell me, how long have you known Matt?"

"'Bout two years, I'd say," Whitmore said.

"And the three of you, have you always hung around together?"

Phil nodded. "Often there'd be four of us, but I'm not seeing anyone right now."

"And where were you this afternoon?"

"I were here, looking after Cheryl. As soon as I heard, I came over. Matt 'n me, we're good friends. Work mates, too."

"And what do you think has happened to him?"

"Same as everyone else, he's either out there minding his own business, or..." Phil examined a spot in the corner of the ceiling above where the cornices joined each other.

"Or...?"

He looked down. "He's gone over," he said quietly, ending on a whisper.

"And how would he do that, an experienced fisherman like him?"

"Could be a number of reasons. Boat could have got into trouble, he could have gone over the side to do a repair, he might have had a funny turn and fallen in. But it might be nothing. He could be out there now, just waiting to be rescued." Phil rocked back on his heels and forced a chuckle.

"Be a coincidence for his radio to go on the blink at the very same time, though wouldn't it?" asked Janice.

Phil pressed his lips together, "Yeah. Yeah, it would."

"Well, thank you, Mr. Whitmore. We'll be in touch. Look after Cheryl, here." Janice closed the door behind her and walked the few steps to the gate that bordered the front of the Crouch's property. The children had gone now. They were probably inside having their tea. As she got into the Gorey Constabulary patrol car, Janice glanced back at the house she'd just left. There was no movement that she could see, just a tortoiseshell cat sitting in the upper window, a net curtain draped across its back. Janice paused, meditating on the cat staring back at her. After a few seconds, she stirred and rapped the car roof with her knuckles a couple of times before getting in and driving off.

CHAPTER TWENTY

THE CREW TOOK some serious convincing, but Barnwell wasn't about to be denied this opportunity to experience something he'd often dreamed of. "I did all the dress-rehearsal stuff the other week in St. Helier," he reminded Brian Ecclestone. "I know what to do. And you'll all be there to yell at me if I get it wrong."

"Okay," Ecclestone finally said. "*If* we find Crouch's boat, we'll winch you down."

Only an officer as popular and as respected as Barnwell would have been given this permission. His successful at-sea rescue of two teenage boys had become the stuff of legend, and his recent exploits, tackling a gun-toting professional hit man and dragging pensioners away from rising floodwaters, had sealed his reputation.

"But the light is failing, and there's still nothing on the radar," Ecclestone added.

Satisfied, Barnwell sat alongside the three other crewmembers who were settled in the chopper's spacious mid-deck. The AW-149 was a big, comfortable helicopter that usually sported fifteen seats, but in this version, the mid-deck mostly provided storage space for stretchers and emergency gear. While they searched for the *Cheeky Monkey*, Barnwell received another briefing on the winch system that would lower him toward the sea, but as the wind picked up, blowing green froth formed from the crests of angry waves, small seeds of doubt started to plant themselves in the constable's mind. It was almost dark, the sea was looking treacherous, and there was still no sign of the—

"Radar contact, bearing one-zero-zero!" a crewman called out.

Barnwell was instantly alert, his concerns forgotten. "Is it the *Cheeky Monkey*?" he asked at once.

Ten seconds were needed to gain a visual on the boat amid failing light. "That's affirm," the voice came from the cockpit. All six crew punched the air, and Barnwell very quickly found himself being attached to the helicopter's powerful winch system.

Crouch's boat was modest, and its discovery among these squalls and increasingly tall waves was as unlikely as it was welcome. But the size of his target presented a huge problem to Barnwell. He would have to land feet-first on the small deck while manually allowing out more cable from the winch via a button on his harness. It was a difficult act of coordination that he'd tried on land in ideal conditions back at St. Helier. Barnwell now recalled with a shiver that he'd made a complete mess of the exercise, and his second time around was only slightly better.

"No movement on board," the pilot called back from the cockpit. Barnwell looked out of the window and down at the boat. He had hoped to see Crouch waving pathetically back at him.

Ecclestone looked through his binoculars, and

confirmed the finding. "Still want to risk it, Constable?" he asked Barnwell, who was now strapped into his harness.

Barnwell took a deep breath. "Ready when you are, lads," the constable replied, sounding more confident than he felt as he double-checked the straps and connections as he'd been taught. Ecclestone nodded to the two-man crew whose task it was to oversee Barnwell's descent, and if necessary, haul him bodily back up to the safety of the helicopter if things went wrong. Neither man relished the idea of a struggling, inexperienced, still slightly overweight police officer, dangling from a swaying cable, fifty feet above a gnarly, wind-lashed sea, in the dark, but it was always a tough situation, no matter who was at the other end of the rope.

The chopper's big searchlight isolated the *Cheeky Monkey* and the AW-149's side door opened, allowing in a shocking gust of freezing air laced with icicles and sea spume. "Remember," a crewman was yelling to him, "keep your arms crossed, and when you hit, keep your feet together." Barnwell felt hands tugging hard at the harness, ensuring that it wouldn't give when subjected to his weight. "If we hit trouble, you'll hear 'Whiskey Oscar' in your headset."

"Wave off, right?"

"Right," the other crewman told him. "It'll mean we're about to haul you back up. Let go of anything, and just let the winch do its job, all right?"

Barnwell nodded, and without further conversation, found that he was perched on the edge of the chopper. A moment later, with a shot of adrenaline that numbed the thinking part of his brain, he pushed himself out of the door to let the winch take his weight as he crossed his arms across his chest. He looked up; the mechanism that was saving him from an unpleasant death was contained within a black box about the size of a big stereo. He could feel and see the cable extend as his descent toward the waves began.

"Lower away!" he heard, his adrenaline building, sending a thrill through his already jacked body. After that, the noise of the chopper's rotors and the raging sea completely took over. The light from the helicopter dazzled him briefly when he glanced down at the small boat, the beam reflecting off the deck. There were still no signs of any movement.

Above him, the pilot was working as hard as he ever had just to keep Barnwell safe. The wind caught the winch line and sent Barnwell into a slow swing like that of a pendulum beneath a clock. The winch system could do little to check the movement. Instead, the pilot mirrored Barnwell's swing, compensating carefully to produce a central point above the *Cheeky Monkey* around which both the chopper and its dangling passenger would move. The winch gave out more cable, foot after foot, and eventually the aircrew felt Barnwell take temporary control as he maneuvered himself down for a safe landing.

Barnwell considered the possibility of dropping into the sea and swimming to the boat, but one glance down at the furious, green waves told him to pay ferocious attention to landing on deck. He had completed no less than five swims of a thousand meters or more, but a calm, warm swimming pool in St. Helier was very different from the roiling, freezing English Channel in November.

The energy driving the swinging motion was now almost entirely spent, and Barnwell found himself staring down past his own feet and onto the deck of Crouch's boat. Feeling heavy and ungainly, he let out more line, which was now suspending him beneath the chopper like a builder's solid, straight plumb line on a construction site, and the roll of the sea brought the deck of the *Cheeky Monkey* up to meet him.

Clunk.

His feet touched down, and he instantly gave out five more feet of cable and grabbed for the metal rail on the ship's starboard side. Reflexively, he knelt and found himself taking deep breaths, relieved to have something solid under his feet. The boat pitched left, and he had to catch himself against the rail to avoid being thrown clear across the deck. Sea spray flecked his face and a wave broke noisily against the starboard side, soaking him instantly in a welter of freezing, green water.

Once some Olympic-level swearing was out of the way, Barnwell got down to business. *Right, lad. Let's get this done and get ourselves home, eh?*

"Matt Crouch!" he called out. "This is Constable Barnwell of Gorey Constabulary. Are you aboard, sir?" Feeling his way along the handrail, Barnwell was able to pull himself level with the pilothouse.

Bugger.

"It's empty," he called up to the chopper. He looked below deck, shining his flashlight wildly around the small space. "There's no one here." The crew was searching the area around the boat using lights mounted on the helicopter's doors, but they too were finding nothing.

"Not your fault, Constable," the airman told him over the radio.

"Yeah."

Inaudible to Barnwell, the crew was receiving a brief but unpleasant lecture from Ecclestone about the perils of staying too long in a dangerous place where they could do no good. "Let's get out of here. He isn't here, so we shouldn't be, either," their commander was telling them. "Money for these things doesn't grow on trees, you know."

"Whiskey Oscar," Barnwell heard through his earpiece. "Brace yourself." Barnwell crossed his arms once more and felt the cable's slack being taken up. As it went taut, there was a strong pull against his chest and torso, and he experienced the unlikely sensation of being physically hauled off the deck of the storm-tossed fishing vessel and back into the rain-lashed air.

"Bloody hell," he muttered. The deck of the *Cheeky Monkey* receded quickly beneath him, but Barnwell was too distracted by the fresh gusts of icy wind that stung his face to pay any more attention to the boat and its missing owner. Then, to Barnwell's distress, the swinging began again, worse than before. He felt like he had become a lightweight toy being passed between two invisible giants, one either side of the helicopter, their game becoming decidedly more violent as the wind picked up and assaulted Barnwell with its brutal, freezing force anew. "Can we hurry this up just a bit?" he asked over the radio. "It's getting a bit 'brass monkeys' out here."

"Roger that," the airman replied, and Barnwell felt a new urgency in his rise toward the oddly shadowy black shape above him. With clouded darkness beyond and the big searchlight finally out of his eyes, Barnwell saw the chopper as a hole in the sky surrounded by lights into which he was being drawn. Flashes of every alien abduction movie he'd ever seen came to mind. Finally, a stern-faced crewman came into view, and he felt strong hands guide him to the ledge by the door. The hands exerted pressure and Barnwell rolled his body inside so that the helicopter door could be closed.

"Well, that certainly cleared away the cobwebs," Barnwell joked.

Ecclestone failed to see the funny side. "I'm glad you enjoyed your little jaunt, Constable, but we did not find Mr. Crouch."

"What will happen now?" Barnwell asked. His hands were too frozen and shaky even to operate his cellphone and call the boss. He needed help disentangling himself from the harness, which in the final moments had begun to pull too tightly in *just* the wrong spot.

Ecclestone leaned back and put his hands behind his head. "I'll send out a launch to bring the boat in. On second thought, let's get one of his mates to bring it in. Weren't a few of them out here searching for him? He looked out of the window. "Maybe that one." He pointed to a blue fishing boat, tiny against the horizon, barely distinguishable against the grey of the sky. Call it up, and let them know," he said to the co-pilot.

"Roger, that," the crewman responded.

Ecclestone turned to Barnwell and said into his headset, "We've got two hours of flying time left. We'll search the water, but if we don't find him soon, it's probably too late."

"Here," a crewman said to Barnwell mildly, reaching over. "Drink this." A mug of steaming coffee arrived by some cherished miracle, and Barnwell spent the next bumpy minutes carefully sipping its life-giving warmth, Ecclestone's words resonating in his ears. *We did not find Mr. Crouch.*

"Commander, I'm not raising that boat. Want me to send out our lads?" The co-pilot was steadily flicking switches on his instrument panel but clearly wasn't having any luck completing Ecclestone's instruction.

"What do you mean, you can't raise them?"

"They're not responding sir."

Ecclestone let out a big sigh, "Oh, all right. But see if you can identify them. I'll have a word when we get back."

Two hours later, they still hadn't found Matt Crouch, and the helicopter and crew headed back to St. Helier. Barnwell radioed ahead and spoke to Graham, giving him the grim news.

"No luck, sir. No sign of him, just his empty boat."

There was a pause, and Barnwell imagined Graham suppressing an oath.

"What on earth has bloody well happened to him, Barnwell?"

"No idea, sir. He seems to have simply vanished. It was like the *Marie Celeste* down there."

CHAPTER TWENTY-ONE

THE NEXT DAY, Barnwell found himself strolling along the boards of the marina, water sloshing gently beneath him. Over his time patrolling the Gorey beat, he had become accustomed to the unstable sensation as he observed the boats and the people that lived and sailed on them. That hadn't been the case when he'd first arrived on Jersey from his native London's inner city beat. Back then, the only unsteadiness he'd known had been the result of a hard night's drinking. Those days were behind him now.

Up ahead, he saw his target. He watched the man kneeling on the wooden slats of the jetty, leaning over to scrub the hull of his boat. It was a small launch, not unlike the one Greg Somerville had gone out in, and by the way the man was punishing it, it was in need of some serious attention.

"Kevin Cummings?"

The man stopped his scrubbing and glanced back before resuming his back and forth, the muscles in his arm showing, the veins standing out.

Barnwell raised his voice, the tenor becoming harder, lower.

"Kevin Cummings." It wasn't a question this time.

Once more, the scrubbing stopped. "Yeah, who wants to know?"

Barnwell sighed. He was a familiar enough sight that he rarely had to produce his ID, but he slipped his fingers into his pocket and pulled his card out, holding it up so that Cummings could see it if he cared to. He didn't.

"I need to speak to you about Greg Somerville."

Cummings leaned back on his haunches, and with resignation threw down his cloth. It was a sheepskin, wet and matted on one side, rough and rubbery on the other. Cummings pushed on his knees to draw himself up to Barnwell's height and regarded him squarely. Drops of water glittered in his beard, while his eyes, beady and suspicious, squinted in the bright sunlight.

"What about him?" Cummings leaned against his boat, and folded his arms. The boat rocked as it bore his weight but he moved with it until it stilled.

"You were in the pub just before Greg Somerville went out on his boat. His body washed up a couple of days later."

"Yeah, I heard."

"I believe the two of you were acquainted. What kind of relationship did you have with Mr. Somerville?"

There was a pause. Cummings pursed his lips. "We were, what I suppose you would call..." He looked up and over Barnwell's shoulder before returning the constable's gaze, "compatriots."

"How so?" Barnwell asked.

"We both wanted the same thing...in effect."

"But?" Barnwell tried.

"But we differed in the way we went about things."

Cummings, looked down at the ground, his arms still folded. He kicked a stone at his feet. It spun into the water.

Barnwell repressed a sigh at Cummings' lack of candor and wearily heaved out a question instead.

"Could you expand on that, sir?"

"I belong to SeaWatch, Officer. We're known as an animal rights group, but really, we're about the environment, the ecology of the sea. We believe in the conservation of sea life in all its forms, but we consider the best way to achieve that is by leaving things alone as much as possible. We intervene only when man corrupts the environment to the extent that the delicate ecosystem is or will be affected if current practices continue."

"So how does that put you at odds with Greg Somerville?"

Again, Cummings paused before he answered. "Greg was a scientist. He was collecting data to understand the migration of the Holden shark. Sounds commendable or at least not controversial until you understand that his constant monitoring was affecting their behavior. He was impeding the very migration patterns he was trying to protect. He was aiming to collect data that would be used to support the sharks in the future, and yet he was distorting how they function. Their displays have evolved over centuries and disrupting them would render his data useless. He was killing his golden goose. His project was a complete waste of time. Worse, it was harmful." More talkative now, Cummings ended his words with a sneer. He leaned his head back, and looked down his nose at Barnwell, waiting for his response.

"So why do you think he continued?"

Cummings lifted his head. "Who knows? Perhaps he didn't see the damage he was doing or recognize the impact it would have on the authenticity of his data. Or more likely, it was a cash cow to him. He didn't want his funding to stop. Research money is difficult to get hold of. Once he'd secured it, he was guaranteed work for years at a time, *and* he got to be a hero. Scientists have big egos, you know? Those egos can get in the way of what's right."

"So you knew him well?"

"We've come into contact over the years. Professionally."

"And what sort of professional activity do you undertake, Mr. Cummings."

"We watch the sea. SeaWatch, get it? As I said, we like to leave things as they are, for the most part."

"But you also said you intervene when necessary. What form might that intervention take, exactly?"

"We lobby local authorities and other governmental agencies over activities we perceive as harmful and which are within their jurisdiction. We sit on the boards of companies whose businesses impact or may impact the surrounding ecosystem. We seek to represent all sea- and ocean-based ecological interests and pledge to go anywhere we feel our voice is needed."

"Do you mount protests?"

"Sometimes."

"And do those protests ever turn violent?"

Cummings pushed himself off the side of the boat and took a step toward Barnwell, his arms by his side now. "Look, I'm not a fool. I can see where you're going with this. We are a peaceful group. I won't deny that tempers haven't frayed in the past, but that's par for the course when you have people as passionate *on both sides* as you have in this game."

"So what was your relationship with Greg Somerville like?"

Kev again looked over Barnwell's shoulder and stared into the distance. He squinted. "It was civil. A little wary, I guess. We were on different sides, remember, but it was cordial. Mostly."

"Nothing physical, then."

Cummings blew air out of his nose in a short, forceful exhale, his head jerking back, a wry smile playing across his lips.

"I wondered how long it was going to take for you to get there." He looked down the gangway briefly before turning back to face Barnwell. "I didn't kill him. That's what you're asking, right? I bumped into him and Tamsin the other morning at the Foc'sle. I was just in the pub for a lunchtime pint. I had no idea they were in there."

"But you knew they were on the island?"

"I had an idea. The Holden sharks are on the move, and Greg and Tamsin have traveled to Jersey for two or three years now to monitor them. It was a reasonable assumption to make."

"So what were your plans?"

"Just to watch, as I said. Their project is legal and aboveboard. We've been unable to persuade the authorities of our viewpoint, so I was here just as an observer."

"And what sort of intervention might you have taken if things hadn't gone the way you thought they should?"

Cummings sighed. "You really don't know how these things work do you?"

"Enlighten me, Mr. Cummings."

"I would have lobbied the powers that be. The local authorities, the Environmental Agency. I might have pressured a powerful local business or two to grease the wheels."

"Seems a rather...peaceful approach."

"That's how these things go. We're not all rabid sabo-teurs, you know, no matter how much the media might portray us as such. Our work can be frustratingly slow at times, but we draw the line at anything physical." Cummings eyes were still piercing and hard, but his voice was even, his body still leaning back languorously against the hull of his boat.

"Ms. Porter said that one of their boats was sabotaged the day before Mr. Somerville went missing. Would you know anything about that?"

Cummings laughed. "Have you listened to anything I've said? We don't go in for that kind of thing. Anyone could have switched out his fuel. The locals weren't too keen on his work. It could just have easily been one of them. But please, go and accuse the local animal activist, eh? We're convenient targets."

Who said anything about switching the fuel?

"So tell me about your interaction with Mr. Somerville in the pub."

"There's nothing to tell. Like I said, I went into the pub for a pint and Greg and Tamsin were there. They seemed to be in a bad mood. I would have been happy to chat, but he wanted none of it, I could tell by his face as soon as he noticed me."

"What did you say to one another?"

"I didn't say much at all. Greg immediately took offense to my presence and warned me off. I didn't want any trouble so I just moved on into the bar. Didn't speak to him again."

"Did you see him leave the pub?"

"No. I ate my lunch at the bar, then went for a walk around town. He'd left by that point. They both had."

"Can anyone vouch for you during the period after you left the bar?"

"People might have seen me wandering around although I don't stick out much. Went to buy a paper and some food at the mini-mart on the front. Someone there might remember me. And I definitely didn't take my boat out that afternoon. You can ask the Harbormaster, if you don't believe me. I didn't see or hear of Greg Somerville again until I heard his body washed up on the beach. I'm sorry about that, but I had nothing to do with it. Now, if you don't mind, I have work to do on my boat."

"Going somewhere?" Barnwell persisted.

"Now that the research has ended, at least until they find someone else to carry on Greg's work, I'm heading back to the mainland."

"Wouldn't now be a good time to increase the pressure on getting the project stopped? Seems like you should be talking to a load of people to get your point across."

Cummings shrugged. "I think that would look a bit insensitive, don't you? Oh, that scientist guy died, let's stomp all over his research and wreck his life's work. Yeah, that wouldn't do our cause any good at all. Chances are, the project will die right along with him. Unless Tamsin takes it over." Cummings bent over and picked up the cloth he had been using earlier. He jumped onto the boat and went inside the pilothouse, effectively dismissing Barnwell. The constable stared at him through the window as Cummings appeared to check his instruments, apparently oblivious to his audience. The constable watched for a moment before looking up and down the floating boards between the boats and, turning on his heel, he made to walk back onto solid ground.

CHAPTER TWENTY-TWO

I T WAS A chilly morning, but without too much
wind. Jean-Luc found himself with time for reflection
as their lumbering boat slowly dragged the magnetometer back and forth along their predetermined search
lanes. The device had a distinctive "ping" which alerted
him to any unusual metallic reading that emanated from the
cold deep beneath them. There had been two false alarms,
perhaps wreckage of ships or aircraft that were destroyed
during Hitler's bid to control the English Channel in 1940,
but nothing that resembled their target.

The dull "thunk" of the cold water against the bow of
the *Nautilus* was rhythmic but disconcerting, a constant
reminder of how poorly their home-away-from-home was
faring in these unpredictable waters. Years of neglect and
hasty hull patches had given her unlovely, bulbous lines,
and she traveled among the waves as though fighting them.
It was one of several frustrations that were threatening to
boil to the surface among the three men onboard.

"Why not just say, 'left' or 'right?'" Hugo had

complained the day before. "It's as much like driving a car as—"

The Parisian was brusquely cut off by a very different accent, the provincial, nasal tones of a working class man from Cherbourg. "We use 'port' and 'starboard' for turns," Jean-Luc had told him, his patience almost exhausted, "and we use 'green' and 'red' for sightings either side of the bow. So, if I'm turning right to follow a sighting exactly half way off the bow, what would I say?" Jean-Luc pressed as if he were a teacher testing a slow student.

Hugo blinked and looked up, calculating his answer before muttering, "Turn to starboard, sighting at red forty-five," he said quietly.

"Exactly. Works the same under water too. *If* we ever get down there." Jean-Luc cast a baleful glance at the two elaborate scuba diving rigs they'd brought along. Specialist dry suits, which kept a warm layer of air between the diver and the freezing water were hanging up. "Any other questions?" Jean-Luc asked. *You egg-headed dummy*, he didn't add.

It was Hugo's accent, his glasses, his style, his painfully obvious lack of knowledge of the sea that caused this schism. Compared to the two veterans, Hugo was young, incompetent, and slow. He knew all this and hated being judged, but reminded himself that the other two men's experience was essential. This was a treasure hunt, not a stag do.

"I think I've got it," Hugo said genially from the pilot-house, unwilling to test Jean-Luc's patience further. They'd tried him in different roles, but ultimately banned him from surveying the equipment. Steering the boat seemed the best role for him. He was kept occupied, and it prevented him from peering over the older men's shoulders.

If they struck gold with their searches, he'd hear about it immediately.

There were long, long stretches of silence on board, with the chugging motor the only soundtrack to this lengthy and frustrating exercise. "Just rumors," his father had insisted of Hugo's idea. "Nothing there but expense and failure," he'd warned. But Hugo wasn't to be put off. He knew a large portion of everything he heard was made up on the spot, of course – mariners love to tell a good story – and much of the rest was hearsay or guesswork, but there was a thread connecting everything he'd heard. Enough people believed the stories that expeditions were planned but later abandoned as enthusiasm and funding to launch them waned. Hugo wasn't letting that happen in his case, nor was he willing for some other team to take all the glory.

He'd traveled to museums to carry out research, sought out translations of books from the time, and studied charts of old wrecks, some discovered only recently. Then, having recruited Victor and Jean-Luc, the three of them had ascertained their search area, and the best timing for their expedition.

Now it was crunch time. There was a narrow window before the winter weather would begin in earnest, and they didn't have much time left. The two older, more experienced men were getting harder to read and ever more grouchy. Neither was interested in getting along beyond the basics, this was purely a mercenary transaction for them.

"Southern leg," he called back, turning to port. The towed magnetometer followed in a broad sweep. He willed for that tell-tale "ping" to come and tell him that he hadn't spent thousands on this hare-brained venture for nothing. He wanted to be *the one* who found it. He wanted the glory, and most definitely the riches; the fabulous, life-changing, never-have-to-work-again riches. There would be TV interviews and magazine articles, maybe even a visit to the Élysée Palace.

Focus, he told himself. This was no time to falter. They were bounty hunters. The prize *would* be theirs.

Barnwell pushed his bike through the doors of the police station and leaned it up against the wall. He took off his helmet and wiped beads of sweat from his forehead. Even in the cool of November after a storm, he could still build up a sweat as he rode around Gorey.

"How'd your little chat with that activist chappie go, Bazza?" Roach asked him.

"Eh, denies seeing Somerville after he left the pub. Says he ate lunch there and wandered around town. Didn't go anywhere near the harbor, he says."

"Do you think he's telling the truth?"

"Seems like he is. His story checks out. Chrissie at the mini-mart remembers him, and the Harbormaster has a record of his boat coming in and not going out again. It's just...Oh, I don't know. He seemed a little too wound up to be willing to toe the softly-softly line he maintains his activist group follows. And he knew about the fuel being switched in Somerville's boat. I'm not sure what to make of him."

There was a big sigh behind him, and he turned.

"Everything all right, Janice?" Barnwell asked.

She was slumped over her computer screen, chin propped in her palm, her lips pursed.

"DI wants me to look at local 'happenings' that occurred after the storm in nineteen eighty-seven, things that seemed odd at first, but which after a time, turned out to have a perfectly reasonable explanation. He wants to pacify Mrs. T.'s overactive imagination. Thing is, I'm not sure anything will settle her down. I think we're trying to fight insanity with logic. She'll think what she wants to think and nothing we're going to say is going to persuade her otherwise."

Barnwell went to check the Constabulary email. "Speak of the devil," he said to the others through gritted teeth. "Eyes left, everyone." He rolled his mouse around, and as the front doors swung open, he looked up and said brightly, "Hello, Mrs. Taylor. What can Gorey Constabulary do you for this fine morning?"

"I told Detective Inspector Graham there would be strange events occurring. The dead scientist, and the missing Matt, and now this." She tapped the large envelope she clasped under her arm. Hearing his name, Graham came out of his office, and she leaned in closer over the reception desk, looking around her in order to check that no one was eavesdropping even though there was nobody present except the police officers. "It's happened again," she confided, her voice low. "Last night."

Graham wondered for a second whether anyone on Jersey had a plate quite as full as his. "What happened, Mrs. Taylor?" he asked, half-ready to tune out her response and think about more important matters.

"I've had another...*visitation*," she said. "I know you'll say I'm cracked, that I've finally gone loopy, but I *know* what I *saw*."

Graham sighed. Barnwell sensed his boss' exasperation and took over, bringing out his iPad. "What exactly did you see, ma'am?"

Mrs. Taylor then described the apparition she'd encountered. By turns, the visitor was "ghostly," "elusive," and "intelligent." It refused to be caught by flashlights. Night after night, according to Mrs. Taylor, it was appearing in the kitchen and causing "a god-awful rumpus." She even had a picture of the being.

A few seconds later, five photographs lay side by side on the reception desk. Barnwell had even rustled up the station's old-fashioned magnifying glass. He handed it to Roach and invited him to apply his forensic mind to this latest mystery.

"Take a load of this, I can't make head nor tail of it."

"It's the camera's flash," Roach said. "It reflects off the pans, the perfectly clean floors, the polished windows." He straightened up and set down the glass. "Just combinations of reflections, that's all."

Barnwell looked again. Mrs. Taylor's normally orderly kitchen was a sea of confusion. Bags of produce had been opened and scattered, and a selection of saucepans and baking sheets were strewn around as if by a malignant kitchen elf. "But what the heck has happened here?" he asked.

Mrs. Taylor had arrived at the station with "proof" of her assertions that she held to be incontrovertible. "It's a poltergeist," she announced, confidently. "An evil spirit, released by the storm."

Graham remained aloof from the group. He kept his own view to himself for the moment; that the pictures showed plenty of inexplicable mess, but nothing else. In the name of community relations, he allowed Barnwell, Harding, and Roach the opportunity to try their hand at solving this particular problem, although he wasn't disposed to let them become too involved. He detected a whopping whiff of the absurd in Mrs. Taylor's own findings.

"Are you sure this mess in your undoubtedly fine kitchen wasn't caused by a hungry guest looking for a snack in the small hours, or a sleepwalking child perhaps? A disgruntled kitchen worker causing chaos on purpose? Really, Mrs. Taylor, an unexplained mystical being seems unlikely," he said, gently.

"I've closed the hotel," Marjorie Taylor told them regretfully. "I can't be sure that my guests are safe until this *visitor* has been chased away or caught."

Roach tried, but ultimately could not resist. "It's tricky, Mrs. T. I mean, what kind of organization deals in this kind of thing?" He stifled a giggle and managed to say, "Who we gonna call?"

Mrs. Taylor rose to her full height and addressed the young sergeant as if admonishing a guest for causing damage to their room. "If there are more *Ghostbusters* jokes on the horizon, young man, I advise you to leave them there. I've heard them all."

Roach reddened and apologized. "Sorry, Mrs. T. It's just so—" he caught sight of the stern look on Mrs. Taylor's face and stopped. Graham took over, guiding the guesthouse owner toward the station's double doors. "I'm going to show these pictures to someone I know in London."

"Oh?" Mrs. Taylor replied, instantly animated at this suggestion of being taken seriously.

"He's something of an expert in... well, *these things*. Give me some time, and I'll see what he comes up with."

"Well, please ask him to hurry. I can't stay closed for long, Detective Inspector. It's my livelihood," Grateful and mollified, at least for the moment, Mrs. Taylor reached the door, buttoned up her winter jacket and checked her slender, antique watch. "Oh, good. I'm just in time for my meeting with that nice journalist, Freddie. He wants to hear all about my *visitations*. Goodbye, David." Graham was so tempted to dash after her and prevent her meeting with Freddie Solomon that he actually took three paces forward. He could already imagine Mrs. Taylor's angry rebuttal. *"I'll speak with whomsoever I choose, young man!"* Any pleading on his part would be fruitless.

He groaned briefly and headed back to his office. "Anyone want my job?" he called over his shoulder before closing the door.

But Janice Harding understood Marjorie Taylor's confusion and distress. Closing down the White House Inn even for a few nights was a measure of her anxiety. Quietly, as the others busied themselves with their pending cases, Janice began to form a plan. She would get to the bottom of the "problem of Mrs. T" and put her out of her misery.

CHAPTER TWENTY-THREE

B Y LUNCHTIME, THERE were around ten people in the library, browsing the stacks or reading in the comfortable chairs around the edges of the room. The midday sun shone through the skylight and found its way into almost every corner of the cavernous space. Laura stopped for a second to appreciate the warm glow emanating from the light reflecting off the wood in the room and wished she could take a picture.

"Goodbye, Mrs. Taylor," Laura said as the older woman passed by the library's distribution desk.

Freddie Solomon had been speaking quietly with Marjorie Taylor at the back of the library, but he had now taken over a good portion of one of the large tables, as had become his custom. It was mostly newspapers today, a selection from just after the Great War, all of them covering wrecks or other mysterious incidents at sea. Laura watched him reading with an avid hunger, all the while taking notes in a thick, black, leather-bound volume. She glanced down as she passed behind him, ferrying some returned books to their rightful places, his handwriting giving the impression that a hummingbird had dipped its wings in ink and then breezily flittered across the page.

On the way back from her re-shelving expedition to the science section, she glanced down again as she passed Freddie's table. "Bermondsey Lighthouse," she said curiously. "I've heard of that place. Out on the islets to the east, isn't it?"

Solomon looked up with a smile and nodded. "Been there for a couple of centuries. But it didn't stop ships from getting into serious trouble." He turned the page of a browned, ninety-year-old newspaper toward her. "Look at this one. The *Genoa Star* was a stout, veteran freighter with a crew of just nine, on perhaps her thousandth voyage from the Swedish ore fields to Gibraltar, and then onto Italy. A storm sprang up in the Channel. Her crew became mystified and then disorientated by the apparently conflicting lights ahead. Before they realized their mistake, the keel of the huge ship hammered into submerged rocks, throwing one person overboard and injuring many."

"Seems straightforward to me," Laura observed, leaning over the old newspaper. "They got themselves off course in bad weather and ran aground."

Freddie raised a finger and gave Laura his I-know-something-you-don't grin. "There was a power cut that night on the island," Freddie told her. "There can't have been lights on the mainland, save for the Bermondsey Lighthouse."

Laura shrugged. "So? The lighthouse beacon should have told them where to steer."

Freddie was practically fizzing with the excitement of it now. "But according to sworn statements by *all nine* of the boat's crew," he explained animatedly, "the lighthouse beacon was in the *wrong place!*" His enthusiasm remained undimmed by Laura's skeptical frown.

"They reported," he said, flipping back through pages of notes, "that the Bermondsey beacon was to their port side."

"That's the left, right?" Laura said.

"Right. The left," Freddie said, grinning again. "But they passed by Jersey to the east, of course, so the light should have been on their starboard side, the *right*."

Laura made to move on but couldn't resist a little parting shot. "I wonder," she asked, waving to an elderly couple as they entered the library, "if they were still dishing out lots of free booze aboard working ships in those days?"

Freddie threw up his hands, but he was smiling. The more scientific, clinical part of him knew that the evidence for the mysterious sea events that he was researching was a little thin on the ground. Heck, some of it was downright *hearsay*. And Laura was right, of course. It wasn't unlike mariners to spin a good yarn and further embellish it with rakish abandon until their world was decorated with fantasies of seductive mermaids and fanciful sea creatures and made more dangerous by spurious mumbo-jumbo about immortality and the Elixir of Life.

But something kept Freddie going. Perhaps, among this collection of half-truths and deliberate falsehoods, there might be something genuinely interesting. Those were the tidbits he craved; the curious, never-before-considered "what ifs" that were so tantalizing. And even if the rumors weren't entirely *true*, a gaudy historical mystery would still make for a simply *splendid* article.

At that moment, his phone buzzed. He looked at it and immediately picked up his satchel. He hurried toward the main entrance, leaving books strewn across the tabletop, waving at Laura as he passed her.

"Enfin, mes amis!"

The green, circular screen of their magnetometer showed exactly the strange, blotchy shape they'd hoped to see when they first set out on this dangerous and stormy quest.

"It could be a massive school of fish," Jean-Luc warned, his eyes glued to the screen. "But I'd bet my house that it isn't. It's at about a hundred and sixty meters." He scanned the screen again. "It's not a definite shape. More like an irregular blur."

Victor wondered aloud, "Underwater explosion?"

"It's possible," Jean-Luc replied, nodding. "Maybe a U-boat that fell foul of the RAF or the British navy."

"A big metallic lump like that would have been found already by now, wouldn't it?" Hugo argued, trying to keep up with the two men's discussion. "There would be records."

But Victor was alert to the impact of the hurricane. He shook his head and flicked his hand in Hugo's direction. "Shush! If the currents were disturbed, even that far down, they might have shifted something. We won't know until we get down there," he said, snorting.

The boat became a busy, noisy place for the fifty minutes it required to set up a major technical scuba dive. "This isn't like what the tourists do," Jean-Luc said when Hugo asked him what was taking him so long. As the lead diver, he began pulling on a two-layer dry suit. Expensive but indispensable, the suit kept a cushion of air between the freezing water of the Channel and the thin, inner layer which hugged his body. Even so, Jean-Luc knew that he was preparing for a very uncomfortable trip down into the deep.

Victor assisted Jean-Luc in donning the cumbersome dry suit and attaching the inflation hoses while Hugo checked the voice and video feeds that led from Jean-Luc's helmet directly to the apparatus on the boat's deck. Once the suit was on, Victor helped Jean-Luc into the harness that contained two specially marked tanks of modified air. These would keep him alive at depth, while two more tanks, slung under his arms and clipped to the suit, would provide additional oxygen for the most difficult part of the trip. "Computer's ready," Jean-Luc reported. Resembling a large wristwatch, his dive computer would feed him data on depth, pressure, and remaining allowed time. Failing to heed its warnings was the short path to serious trouble. At these depths, he'd have a very limited amount of time to look around – perhaps only ten minutes – but the entire dive would take nearly four hours. "And I'm ready for the helmet," he added.

Victor slid the heavy helmet over his fellow explorer's head and locked it into place. Jean-Luc's view of the world was now through dense glass, but it was the only way to survive in such extreme conditions. A large flashlight hung from his suit, along with a range of safety equipment and a small, yellow spare oxygen tank. Weights that would act as ballast were strapped around his waist. There was even a knife designed for underwater work. Jean-Luc knew that it was the season for Holden sharks to migrate, and though they were mostly docile, he didn't relish the possibility of an encounter with such a massive beast.

Once everything was double-checked, Jean-Luc waddled heavily to the port rail of the ship.

"I really, *really* wish we didn't have to do it like this," Hugo complained. They were on an old fishing boat, not a specially rigged dive vessel. Jean-Luc would simply have to jump over the side and into the Channel. "All set?"

"Wish me *bonne chance*!" Jean-Luc said, and with a tap

of all his equipment, a superstitious ritual he went through prior to every dive, he slung a leg over the rail and tipped himself gracelessly into the cold water with an impressive splash.

Below the surface, once the confusion of his entry cleared, all was quiet and calm. He tested his breathing apparatus. At Jean-Luc's insistence, Hugo had splurged on the latest design, a re-breather that funneled spent air into a filter and then to his helmet. It would extend his dive time and eliminate exhalant bubbles. It was working fine. He checked that the line connecting his suit to the boat was secure and then steadily decompressed, allowing a stream of air out from his suit so that he would lose buoyancy and steadily sink into the murk.

Jean-Luc kept both eyes glued to his dive computer. He could descend at any speed he wanted, but once the sunlight that filtered through the upper reaches of the water penetrated no further, the visibility would plummet. There would be no way to see the bottom or his precious target, and he would rely solely on the readings from his dive computer. He flicked on the powerful flashlight. Immediately, it illuminated a tiny shrimp that fled from him; it was the only movement in this still, outlandish place.

Thirty meters. Most recreational divers would go no further, but Jean-Luc dropped past this point, sliding down into the abyss until he passed fifty meters, then sixty. The darkness became complete, save for the cone of rough visibility provided by his flashlight. The water became clogged with silt and mud, a dense soup that yielded nothing. Once his computer read a hundred meters, he called up to the surface.

"Proceeding normally. One hundred. Viz is bad, no surprise there."

"Roger," Victor replied quietly, Hugo listening over his shoulder. Their interactions would be minimal, at Jean-Luc's request. He was a solo explorer now, navigating through a strange and pitiless place. He wanted to focus. A fish approached him, small and silver but retreated in a lightning blur as though the human form were a predator.

"One thirty. No sign of the bottom yet." He continued to descend through the murky gloom.

The stress began at around a hundred and forty meters. The pressure of the water on Jean-Luc's body brought along with it a companion pressure, defensive psychology cleverly designed by eons of evolution to divert him from his purpose. He recognized the feeling, a slight tightness in his chest, the urge to breathe deeper, even to gasp for air. There was a tiny voice, nagging at him: *You shouldn't be here. You're trespassing.* Then it started to undermine him. *Tons of crushing water exists above you. How long will it take to even reach the sweet, fresh air at the surface? How easy would it be to never experience that again?*

But Jean-Luc was a veteran of these depths and mastered his emotions after a few moments. With his breathing under control once more, he felt a new surge of confidence, reminding himself that he was permitted only a brief visit to this underwater world and should make the most of it.

"One hundred fifty," he said into his helmet. "Cold, but doing okay."

Jean-Luc had passed into water that was only a few degrees above freezing. Without his dry suit, he would have succumbed in moments.

His flashlight caught something, and Jean-Luc immediately added air to his suit to kill his downward momentum. Hovering at a hundred and fifty-five meters, he turned slowly in a circle to locate the object that he instinctively knew didn't belong in this eerie other-world. He unhooked his flashlight and began a search pattern. He needed to find it quickly. His dive computer was adamant. He had only twelve minutes left before he would have to head back up again. Ignoring the computer would mean risking a dangerous buildup of compressed nitrogen in his blood. If it later formed bubbles as he ascended, they would expand and cause several days of the most excruciating joint pain.

There you are. He began to make out pieces of debris, odd-shaped and strewn haphazardly along the seabed. "Okay," he told his two colleagues, waiting patiently above him, "I've got wooden pieces of some kind." He knew this would excite his fellow treasure seekers: U-boats weren't made of wood. This, apparently, was something else.

He surveyed the debris field, trying to ascertain where the pieces were more numerous. "More debris to the north," he said. "Larger pieces... And... Wait..."

He swam for the first time now, his long fins taking him steadily northward as he shone the light down onto the seabed, perhaps four meters below him. "More large pieces," he said. Then his colleagues heard Jean-Luc give an unexpected gasp of the most complete surprise.

The experienced diver continued his slow journey over the debris field. His own eyes were now struggling to make out in detail the source of his surprise. It was something that had no earthly business among the sinuous, worn curves of underwater topography: *a straight line.*

His dive computer told him that he had only six minutes before he needed to start his ascent to the surface. Kicking harder, he propelled himself forward until he found the incongruous piece that was bothering his subconscious, a long timber that lay at odds with the other pieces. Then, there was another, by itself to the right, and another to the left.

"Five minutes remaining. I've got wooden debris and timbers," he reported. Thirty seconds later, he was hovering over a large collection of beams, radiating out from a central point. He allowed a tiny sip of air from his suit and descended until he was within a meter or so of it.

"I confirm that I have a shipwreck," he said. "A large, wooden sailing ship. That's my first estimate." He could imagine his colleagues' unadulterated jubilation up above, but they'd achieve nothing if he didn't complete the dive safely and return to tell the tale. "Three minutes only. I'm going to see if I can find the cargo hold."

It didn't take long. The reason for this mighty ship's final journey was laid bare, there amid the wreckage. And as Jean-Luc shone his flashlight into the wrecked, decayed hold of the ship, finding its timbers split and askew but the cargo still within them intact, he hovered, suspended in the dark depths, cocooned in his glassy, insulated world. And then he let out a big whoop of joy.

CHAPTER TWENTY-FOUR

D ETECTIVE INSPECTOR GRAHAM allowed himself to worry for just a few moments on whether he was facing the first genuine public order crisis of his career.

Gorey's marina was the scene of an ever-increasing large and noisy protest. It seemed to Graham as though everyone who'd ever called themselves a fisherman was showing up. There were boats from all over the Channel Islands, from the larger Jersey and Guernsey, as well as the smaller Alderney and tiny Sark. Dozens of mainland-based boats were also arriving, showing their solidarity with their fellow fishermen on the island. Their boats crammed the harbor until it looked like the set of a Hollywood movie about the Little Ships of Dunkirk. Neither Graham nor Barnwell would have ever believed such a sight was possible.

As Barnwell drove them over the rise and into town, they began to see the extent of the gathering. "Bloody hell fire," Barnwell exclaimed. He turned to his boss who looked less taken aback than simply exhausted by the thought of the fracas to come. "Are we being invaded by the Germans again, sir?"

Graham took a deep breath and straightened his tie. "Worse, I'm afraid, Constable. By Des Smith and his pals." Graham reached for his phone.

"Stone the crows. Will the Navy be able to cope, or do you think we'll need a special meeting of the UN Security Council?" Barnwell said as he gave a quick blast of the police siren prompting the dawdling pedestrians that were obstructing their path to jump out of the way.

Roach answered Graham's call.

"Close the station if you have to, lad, but I need all of us down at the marina." Graham thought for a second. "You'll have to drive by the Kerry Center and pick up Janice. And Sergeant?"

"Sir?"

"Try to keep a straight face."

"How do you mean, sir?" Roach asked.

"Because," Graham spelled out, "you're going to be hauling Sergeant Harding out of her hatha yoga class."

"Crikey." Roach imagined the scene.

"Just give her a few moments to finish chanting or whatever one does at those things, and get her straight in the car, okay?"

"Righto, sir," Roach said.

Barnwell found a parking place by the baker's. "Shall I call the armed response unit, sir? Helicopters?"

Graham wasn't in the mood. "I hope you're taking this seriously, Barry. There are people in newspaper offices and parliamentary meeting rooms who are going to be discussing in detail what happens here today."

"Sir?" Barnwell asked as they headed through a curious and growing crowd toward the marina itself.

"Anglo-French relations hinge on the amicable resolution of disputes like this one," he explained, leaning into Barnwell so that he could keep his voice low. "Quotas and fishing areas are hot-button issues. Mix them up with a lot of anger and more than a few spoonfuls of grief, and we've got a powder keg ready to blow. We need to keep a lid on this. And *definitely* avoid any kind of violence." He turned to the constable just as Barnwell raised his voice to the very edge of courtesy in a bid to hurry people along. "So, no antagonism, all right?" he said, sheltering his ears from Barnwell's commands.

"Right, sir," Barnwell replied at a less ear-threatening volume. "I'd feel better if we had some backup, though," he added. "In case things get nasty."

Graham feigned confidence. "These fellas? They're angry, but they're not criminals. Isn't that what you told me earlier? Like family you said."

"I said a 'warring family.' And I think it all very much depends," Barnwell told him, "on how far down the bottle Des Smith has proceeded."

It wasn't a pleasant prospect. Barnwell could still recall the colorful verbal assault Des had inflicted upon him and Roach when they'd locked him up three years ago. "Let's just see what's going on," Graham said, puffing now. "And try to prevent Des Smith and his friends from re-starting the Hundred Years War."

Down at the marina itself, the air was thick with klaxons, shouts, chants, and howls of protest. Perhaps a hundred and fifty fishermen were there, supported by at least as many friends and family. Curious onlookers doubled that number. It was nearing low tide, and the beach that spread off to the right of the marina was crowded as though it were the height of summer. But these visitors were not there to catch some rays, they were there to make a point. They were standing, holding signs, sitting in circles, and milling about as though waiting between acts at a music festival.

"Hands Off Our Fish!" was the second most common sign, behind, "Justice for Matt" and similar pleas. The crowd seemed to comprise three different groups, each led by a speaker who was either whipping them up with call-and-response routines or lecturing them about the situation. From what Graham could hear, only some of this information was valid. Mostly, he heard ill-advised accusations and an upwelling of stormy anger that worried him as much as any hurricane.

"Sir, look," Barnwell said, tugging his boss' arm. Behind them, a TV crew had somehow found a place to park their big blue and white van and was setting up for what appeared to be a live broadcast.

"Oh, cripes," Graham observed. "Things are going to get dangerously busy here, once the word reaches around the whole island."

"The whole *country*," Barnwell warned. "We're going to be on the *Six O'clock News*, boss." He pulled out his phone and ran his finger from the bottom to the top of the screen. "And look, Mr. Solomon has been busy."

The blogger had somehow cobbled together a short piece entitled, "The Gorey Marina Revolution," which encouraged everyone to join the protest and make their voices heard.

Graham said nothing. He continued through the crowd but then stopped and spent a long moment just looking around, taking in the scene. In addition to the fishermen, there were fathers with children on their shoulders, small groups of teenagers with their bicycles, elderly couples curious to see what was going on, and a general surge of people toward the beach and the marina. He guessed that the crowd would reach eight hundred, maybe a thousand in the next half-hour, and with such numbers in close proximity, even if the tide was low, they were facing a serious safety problem. And that was quite aside from the public order issue that Graham feared might suddenly flare.

"We've got to get in there and talk to Smith," he said, pulling Barnwell with him through the crowd. "He's at the center of all this, and he can defuse it."

But reaching Des Smith required a Herculean effort. Members of the press, both professional and amateur photographers, and of course, Freddie Solomon, whom Graham had silently come to refer to as "that odious runt," were crowding around the old fisherman and his cohort, all willingly receiving the Smith's view of the situation. "It's piracy, I'm telling you!" the old man was roaring. "Piracy on the high seas. Unfair restrictions and fish fiddling, ladies and gents, you mark my words!"

Graham swore under his breath but then saw what needed to be done. "Right." He muttered his instructions to Barnwell as they cleared the crowd immediately in front of them and strode more easily toward Smith's group.

"Afternoon, Des," Graham said quietly in his ear. "Might I have a word?" Smith was a practical man, and bore the Detective Inspector no ill will. "Hang on a minute," he said ungraciously to the crowd of protesters, press, and onlookers. He turned his back on them to speak with Graham. He glanced up at the towering Barnwell. "All right, Barry." Then, to the DI, "I see you've brought muscles with you, in case there's trouble."

Graham gave him an affable smile. "Oh, I'm not too worried about that. Bit of a crush on the beach, though, wouldn't you say, Des?"

"Aye," the old man replied.

"Lots of kids here today, too," Barnwell added. "Last thing we'd want is for anyone to get separated, or…"

"You want us to pack up and go home?"

I wouldn't say no. "I'm here to broker an agreement," Graham announced. "I need you to get your men to disperse, Des. This is a public order problem. It's dangerous."

"Oh yeah? Well, we need to be heard."

"Look, why don't I get you some airtime with the TV crew? That way, you can speak in an orderly, coherent manner. You'll get your message across much more effectively that way and to a wider audience too. You'll be on the *Six O'Clock News*, a national platform. And I'll see if I can get the mayor down here."

Smith weighed this up and then turned to his cohort. A few moments' mumbling and one or two objections later, Smith turned back and gave Graham a nod. "All right. You've got a deal. But I want a word in private with you, Mr. Graham. There's something you need to know."

They spoke on board Smith's boat, alone and out of earshot. When Graham returned, he promptly rallied Barnwell, and they headed back up the hill to the car. As they trudged up the slope, they passed a journalist they both recognized from one of the national news shows going in the opposite direction. He was accompanied by a cameraman.

"How did you do it, sir?

"Oh, I just gave them a call. The media are always desperate for stories to fill up their slots. The public at large think it's a big deal to be on the telly, but it's nothing special, not really. I was on it plenty of times in my old job. The mayor's on his way, too."

Fifteen minutes later, Graham and Barnwell were

finally back in the car, taking the gently meandering country road out of town and toward the Constabulary. Smith, for his part, had asked his men to quietly advise the onlookers that the show was over for today, and within ninety minutes, Roach and Harding would report that the marina and beach had returned to some semblance of their usual calm and purpose.

But Barnwell could see that Graham was perplexed. On the drive back, he seemed to be muttering to himself while working something out in his head. "This just got a lot trickier," he said.

"How's that, sir?" Barnwell asked.

"It's these two cases. I just...Well, I just don't know." He lapsed back into a thoughtful silence.

"So, sir, what did he tell you? Des Smith."

"I listened to his daft theories about the French and reassured him we were doing everything we could. He did extract a promise from me to go out searching for Matt Crouch's body again, though. I guess that can't hurt, although I'm anticipating an almighty battle with Ecclestone. But now I have another thing on my mind. Smith told me that if we prove French involvement in either case, he's going to rally the fishing boats and blockade a major French harbor."

"Crikey," Barnwell breathed. "We can't have that kind of thing."

"No, we can't," Graham said. He quite literally shuddered to think of the implications.

As Barnwell drove, Graham made the tricky call to Brian Ecclestone. Despite the Jersey Coastguard's recent liaisons with the Gorey Constabulary, this was the first time the two men had spoken.

"Not a chance," was the commander's first response to

Graham's request that he again search the area where Matt's boat was found, but as the Detective Inspector's temper audibly rose, and the commander felt real pressure to be "one of the team," he begrudgingly relented. "I'll dispatch the SAR fixed-wing aircraft for a two-hour search. All the latest electronics gadgets," he promised.

CHAPTER TWENTY-FIVE

G RAHAM WAS GOING through his "end of day" routine, clearing his desk and making a new list of tasks for the next day, when the phone rang.

"David? Brian Ecclestone." The background noise immediately told Graham that Ecclestone was onboard a helicopter.

"Evening, Brian. What's new?" He grabbed his notepad, hopeful that this wasn't a call that would lead to a reprimand for wasting precious Coastguard funds on a wild goose chase.

"We're out here, as you requested, searching the area where Crouch's boat was found."

"Any luck?"

"Not yet, but I'm sending you the same image that we're seeing here," he explained. "It's a reading from the seabed. It makes absolutely no sense."

Graham quickly pulled up the email on his laptop. Ecclestone had sent him a sonar picture. "Looks like a...

Well, I'm not an expert," he admitted, "it could be the Loch Ness Monster for all I know."

Ecclestone found this pretty funny, and Graham heard him genuinely laugh – not a sneer or derisive chortle, but a full-throated, humorous laugh. "It's not Nessie," he replied. "But it's dense, solid, *and* fragmented, which is strange, almost like something's broken up. It's large, too. That's all we can say for now. It's in the area north of where Crouch's boat was found and west of where Somerville's body was recovered."

"And you're saying this thing might have had something to do with those cases?" Graham asked. It sounded far-fetched, even as he said it, but he fervently hoped this was the reason for Ecclestone's call.

"We can't know for sure. It's simply an oddity. Something we wouldn't expect to see. And so for that reason, I thought you should know," Brian replied. "My guys are saying it's not a submarine. No sign that it's a conventional wreck either, and there's nothing on the charts to explain what it might be."

Graham waited for some kind of *denouement* to this story. "So...What do we need to do?"

Ecclestone let him down. "Nothing, for now. We need more readings."

Graham said it for him. "Costly."

"Exactly. Now, I've got to go. We're about to buzz a fishing boat that's where it shouldn't be. Looks like it might be the one young Barnwell gave a good talking to the other day."

After he ended the call, Graham closed his office door and spent half an hour in total silence, letting his mind work on the available evidence of the two cases in front of him. He was alone at the station. He had directed Sergeants

Roach and Harding to remain down at the marina until the end of their shift. Barnwell was taking some personal time before he started his overnight duty.

The two cases were troubling Graham. He could appreciate just how easily rumors of fantastical beasts and paranormal events could become so popular. The idea that someone had deliberately targeted two unassuming men while they were about their work *at sea* was so problematic that he had trouble seriously contemplating it. The fact that there had been two unexplained misadventures inside a few days, however, forced him to do so. He considered the angles.

Tamsin seemed genuinely grief-stricken. While her romantic troubles with Greg were fraught, even if she had chased after Greg that afternoon, she had returned far sooner than was likely to effect a murder. Graham twirled his pen around his fingers and thought further. It was possible that Tamsin had come across him very quickly, however. They really had no idea at what point in his afternoon or where exactly Greg had met his death and it certainly wouldn't be the first time a grieving girlfriend had ultimately proved a murderer.

Graham's other theory, that a fisherman had confronted Greg for disrupting his livelihood or some other reason, felt weak too, and still left him attempting to explain Matt Crouch's disappearance. They had nearly completed their interviews with all the boat owners who were out the afternoon of Somerville's disappearance, and while several of them didn't have alibis, they all denied seeing him. And who was to say there wasn't, as Des kept asserting, a French or other international boat out on the water that they knew nothing about? He thought back to the boat Barnwell had remonstrated with, the one that was "lost." Boats and ships passed through the Channel all the time. It was like Piccadilly Circus out there at times. They had no way of knowing exactly who traveled on through.

Graham sighed. Even the animal activist checked out. He started to feel hopeless and reflected on the point at which he might decide to "re-prioritize" the active investigation into the two cases. An icy chill ran through him when he considered the impact that news would have on the local people, especially the fishermen.

Graham sat back and stretched his tense back muscles, reaching up toward the office ceiling and letting out a long sigh of frustration. He glanced at his phone. There was a brief yelp of despair when he saw four texts, all from Laura. He called her at once.

"So, how was your 'public order problem?'" she asked, glossing over his graceless habit of remaining *incommunicado*.

"Complete madness," was his description of the situation at the marina. "Dangerous and disorganized. But I think we found a solution. How were things at the library?"

"Quiet. Freddie was poking around again, until someone called him about the protest. He left without even packing up his things."

"Salacious headlines don't write themselves," Graham mumbled. "He's got a lot to answer for."

"Oh, he's harmless. And isn't it good for those in power to be held accountable?"

"He's not even a real *journalist*, for heaven's sake," Graham said, narrowly keeping the frustration out of his voice.

Laura let the topic drop, and focused instead on when she might have the chance to actually lay eyes on the DI, at long last. "Any chance I'll see you for dinner? I'm dipping into my grandmother's cookbook again."

Somehow, Graham mustered the emotional processing power to simultaneously juggle two unyielding cases, three subordinates, and a remarkable woman who simply wanted to cook him a meal. It was a feat almost beyond him, but he was determined not to be defeated. "I promise," he said, knowingly boxing himself in. "Seven o'clock, your place."

Energized by the thought of an evening with Laura, and now constrained by his own commitment, Graham drank a whole pot of tea in twenty minutes. He reveled in the rocket-fuel caffeine boost and very quickly dealt with five separate phone calls.

He spoke first with Sergeant Harding for an update. She assured him that the marina was returning to a relative quiet, and that Smith and his boys had suspended their protest. "They even asked people to take their litter away," Harding told him. "As protests go, that one went. Most of the non-local boats have returned home except for a few whose crews have infused the local economy with purchases down the pub."

The second phone call was one he took from the local newspaper. Graham gave them a quote that struck a balance between his desire for public calm and his understanding of the fishermen's grievances. He finished with a solemn promise to do all in his power to catch those responsible for the murder of Greg Somerville and disappearance of Matt Crouch, whomever they might be. He was, however, mindful to follow the first rule of dealing with women, children, and the press: *Don't make promises you can't keep.*

Then he called Barnwell to confirm their plan to have the constable keep an eye on the marina overnight, just in case Smith and his fellow rebels decided to wake up Cherbourg Harbor at four in the morning with some ill-advised demonstration. "I'll put the station phone on forward to yours when I leave."

He also called his superior to report on events at the marina and his two cases. He assured the Chief Constable that the situations were under control. "No need, sir," Graham assured him, when offered additional assistance, including specialist riot police. "Let us have seventy-two hours, and we'll be in a better position. Might even have a result by then."

The more senior man agreed, but warned Graham against biting off more than he could chew. "Even the very best," he said, intimating that he felt DI Graham was in just this category, "need a little help from time to time."

"Thank you, sir."

His final phone call was to Laura. "See you in ten minutes." He turned out the lights in his office and headed past the deserted reception desk to lock up the main doors and switch on the lighted sign that instructed callers what to do in the case of an emergency. The desk phone rang, but he ignored it. After three rings, it stopped as it switched over to Barnwell's mobile. It rang again as he was setting up the coffee machine, something he always did for the night shift cover. The temptation to pick it up was nearly overwhelming, but some minutes later, as she welcomed him into her small cottage that smelled of Roma tomatoes and sizzling garlic, Laura Beecham discovered that David Graham was as good as his word.

A mile away from Laura's home, Barnwell was cycling to the marina under a moonlit sky when his mobile rang. He braked and put his foot down on the ground to answer it. As he listened, he quickly pulled out his notebook and started writing furiously, cradling the phone under his ear, leaning on his handlebars to write. "Right. Right. Stripe, you say? Three miles north. Got it. We'll check it out, sir. Thank you for phoning in." He ended the call and immediately dialed Roach's number. "Somerville's boat's washed up. Check with the boss, but I think you'd better get yourself up there sharpish."

Barnwell rung off and hooked his foot under his pedal, slotting his phone into his jacket's breast pocket. He made to push off before stopping and pulling his phone out again to send a text.

On second thoughts, don't check with the boss. He's busy.

CHAPTER TWENTY-SIX

LAURA GATHERED UP the two empty dinner plates from the table. "I guess that was okay, then?" she smiled.

"Delicious," Graham replied. "Your grandmother was quite the chef. But you didn't have to go to any trouble on my account. Leftovers would have been fine."

He looked very different in a casual button-down shirt and jeans, and Laura found him a lot more relaxed and seemingly able to set aside the day's investigative travails than he had on previous occasions. "It's no bother, really. I wanted to," she explained. "Well, maybe I was showing off for you," she admitted with a small smile. "Just a little."

Graham checked his phone. There was a text from Roach.

Albatross washed up. Doing prelim forensics. Not much. A bit of damage to the paintwork, maybe a collision. Everything else looks tickety-boo.

Graham sighed and tucked his phone away, determined to enjoy his evening.

Laura motioned for Graham to join her on the couch.

There was no TV in her cottage. Instead, virtually every bit of wall space was crammed with shelving containing books of all shapes and sizes. Though Graham hadn't been upstairs yet, Laura had told him that most of her personal library was kept there. "You haven't talked about your cases today," she noted.

"Well, things are at a bit of a standstill," he admitted. "We've got a small crowd of suspects but no way to really eliminate or move forward with any of them."

Laura sat up and folded her legs under her before reaching out to take Graham's hand. "Tell me," she said mildly. "You never know, I might be able to crack the case."

"I wish you would!" Graham replied, laughing. "Someone needs to. And with what I have at the moment, I don't know if it's going to be me."

"Of *course* it will be," Laura told him. "Just like the other times. Tell me the details, and let's see if I can help."

Graham laid out the facts of the case. "Our first victim argued with his girlfriend, went out on his boat, and was struck with an unidentified object. The blow or blows killed him, and he either fell or was pushed overboard. His body washed up a few days later. A couple of days after he was last seen alive, our second victim, a fisherman, goes out to look for our first victim's boat, which hadn't washed up. He doesn't return. The second victim's boat is found empty, there's no evidence, no body, and now the whole fishing community is distraught, up in arms, and developing conspiracy theories."

"And they're blaming the French, thinking it's all to do with quotas and such," Laura summed up. "Is that possible, do you think?" She reached for her glass and took a sip of wine. It was exceptionally robust and fruity.

"Sure," Graham replied. "It's just entirely without

precedent, and there's simply no evidence to support such an idea. You have to understand that around here, if there's something awry, the French are always going to get the blame. Des Smith has got the fishermen so worked up that they're allowing their opinions to run roughshod over the facts."

"So, can we rule them out, the French fishermen, I mean?" Laura asked.

"There's no evidence to rule them in, and there's no evidence to rule them out," Graham told her. "Another idea is that one of the local fishermen killed the two men. We've spoken to them all now. About twenty don't have alibis, but no real motive. Again, there's no evidence pointing the way. There are a couple of other people I can't rule out completely. Tamsin, Somerville's girlfriend, of course. She's still the prime suspect, though we've nothing concrete. The timing doesn't fit."

"And someone else?" Laura asked.

"Yeah. Somerville had a turbulent relationship with a local green who was here 'observing' him. They had history. His alibi checks out, but Barnwell thinks he may have been involved in sabotaging Somerville's boat in the days leading up to his disappearance." Graham fell silent before springing back to life. "We still don't know if the Somerville and Crouch cases are connected or even that Crouch is dead. For all we know, he could be living the high life somewhere on the Cote D'Azur." Graham ran a hand through his hair.

"So," Laura said after a pause, "what will you investigate tomorrow?"

Graham looked at her with a kind smile. "We really don't have to talk about this, you know," he said. "It's only work." Both knew this to be a remarkable understatement.

"I think it's fascinating," Laura said. Their hands were still entwined, and his felt warm and powerful within her slender fingers. "But I'm sorry you're frustrated. There just seems to be something missing, doesn't there? A part of the case that you haven't seen or understood yet."

Graham mulled this over. Ordinarily, he'd have bristled at such an observation, but she was right. "It's all just so strange," he said. "And I haven't even begun to tell you about Mrs. Taylor's ghostly ghoul or today's unusual find on the seabed." He went quiet for a long moment. "Hang on."

Laura watched him thinking. His lips moved slightly, and his eyes flitted from one invisible object to another as if comparing two antique vases to see which one was fake.

"Hang on a minute," he said again, absent-mindedly.

Laura said nothing. Perhaps this was how it was for Mozart in those moments when a new concerto popped into his head, fully realized, transcription-ready. His mental mechanisms were working overtime, and Graham seemed oblivious to the present moment, even when, after four minutes of complete silence, Laura gently squeezed his hand in an attempt to bring him back from wherever he'd gone.

It all clicked into place. "Bloody hell," Graham muttered. He stood suddenly. "Laura Beecham, you're a genius." He leaned down to kiss her, then announced, "Damn. Laura, I'm sorry. I have to go."

"Now?" she asked, largely hiding her disappointment. She stood with him and helped him gather his things.

"Yeah, I'm sorry," he said again. "But you've been truly helpful." He found his jacket and was heading to the door before he remembered to return and kiss her again, harder this time. "It's just that I hadn't put together the, um... " The idea was yet too hazily formed for words. "Yeah. I've got to go," he said finally.

Laura watched him through the window. A distracted amble became a purposeful stride, and by the time he reached the end of Campbell Street, the Detective Inspector was jogging purposefully toward the Constabulary. Laura turned away to survey the detritus of their meal and looked at the clock. It was still early. She went to a drawer and pulled out a roll of aluminum foil. Unfurling a length, she covered the leftovers of their dinner, taping the dish at the sides. She shrugged on her coat and left her cottage, heading in the direction of town. It was dark and the evening was cold, but the smell of the still-warm leftovers energized her. Her grandmother's cannelloni was delicious. Billy and his mum would love it.

CHAPTER TWENTY-SEVEN

S ITTING SIDE BY side, opposite the sliding door of the powerful Royal Navy helicopter, Barnwell and Graham exchanged a glance and each found that the other was smiling.

"You'll be getting used to this," Graham joked. "*Barry Barnwell: Man of Action*. I can imagine the book launch now."

Barry wasn't as confident as he looked, but his recent frozen, harrowing descent on to the *Cheeky Monkey* had at least reassured him that only crew who knew what they were doing took to the skies. This team was comprised of members who were all highly experienced with years of service behind them. They had a female pilot and co-pilot, and in the helicopter's cabin, a male loadmaster. These were Royal Navy personnel, not Coastguard or volunteers, and the helicopter they were in certainly wasn't one belonging to the search-and-rescue service.

"Flight time is about seven minutes," the loadmaster told them. Headsets with microphones allowed them to talk without yelling in this noisy space. "Please be advised that this is a no-smoking Lynx helicopter. Just sit back and relax. Can I get anybody a drink? A cocktail, perhaps?" he joked.

"Make mine a stiff double," Barnwell muttered to Graham.

"If I'm right about this, I'm buying. All night," his boss replied. "Just keep your fingers crossed, all right?"

Barnwell comically crossed all his limbs and grinned. "How on earth did you come up with this anyway, sir?"

With a slight shrug, Graham succinctly explained the "lightbulb" moment that had unfortunately interrupted yet another evening with Laura. He ended with, "It just came to me."

The chopper lurched slightly as the pilot adjusted the flight path.

"I'm just trying to picture it, sir," Barnwell said. "You're there, last night, having dinner with someone, and then everything just stops, and you're suddenly dashing down the road to the station?"

Graham grinned sheepishly. "Yeah, that's about right. Laura, my dinner partner, was very understanding, but I'm really trying not to make a habit of it."

Barnwell tried not to smile at the fact that he'd just smoked out a major personal admission from his boss.

"It was those strange readings that Ecclestone called in," Graham explained. "I mean, the Channel is full of wrecks from the last thousand years, and with that French boat hanging around out there, where it shouldn't be, I just put two and two together."

"French boat, sir?"

"Ecclestone told me it was still around, the one you warned off."

"But wouldn't the simplest logic have led us to Tamsin?"

"It would, but we can't link any evidence to her, and her window of opportunity to commit a murder was very tight. No, I don't think Tamsin killed anyone. I believe that her grief was genuine and that she was as honest with us as her mental state allowed."

"And we can strike Des Smith and his friends off the list too?"

Raising his voice slightly, even with the microphone to help, Graham replied, "I think so, don't you?"

"I can't see it, sir. I just can't."

"Everyone else's alibis checked out; Kev Cummings and the French fishermen. I felt we had to look elsewhere, and then it hit me. I spent the rest of the evening double-checking my thinking and then called up one of my oldest friends."

When they left school, David Graham and Paul Connolly had both swapped their school uniform for a different kind. In Connolly's case, he now wore a whole armful of gold braid as a Royal Navy Commander. As such, he was in a position to honor unusual requests at short notice, including ordering the little military operation Graham and Barnwell were now essentially leading.

"She's actually steaming her way south to join three other vessels for a Royal event on the Thames," Connolly had told him the night before. "But I've redirected her to your patch, and she'll dispatch her Lynx to St. Helier and pick you up." Now the two men found themselves aboard the powerful helicopter as it cruised north toward her parent ship, *HMS Northumberland*. Barnwell was the first in the cabin to spot it, a wall of steel and iron atop the water, bristling with threat.

"Bloody hell, boss. What have you gone and done?"

Graham leaned over to observe the aquiline shape of

the warship beneath them as they banked for their final landing approach. "Nice, isn't she?" he quipped.

Barnwell was gripped. "I thought you meant some little minesweeper, or a fisheries patrol ship. This is a...Actually, what is it?" he asked the loadmaster.

"Type 23 Frigate," he announced. "One of these could take on a submarine wolf pack and protect the fleet from enemy aircraft, all at the same time."

"Crikey," Barnwell gasped. "That's a lot of firepower, sir."

Graham was grinning as though it were his birthday. "Well, I told Paul I was serious. I can't imagine anyone giving us any trouble once this bloody great thing thunders into view."

"Brilliant," Barnwell smiled.

"Brace, please," the loadmaster told them just as the helicopter was finishing its "flare," shedding some final knots of speed before settling down on the frigate's flight deck. The loadmaster jumped up but motioned for them to stay in their seats while the rotors slowed and stopped.

"Right. If you'll follow me, please?"

Graham and Barnwell jumped down. They were briskly escorted from the gusty flight deck that dominated the rear of the warship, through a metal hatchway, and down a maze of corridors. The loadmaster whisked them along as if late for something, and Graham shortly saw why as they arrived at a small mess hall with dining tables and a serving counter, but no diners.

"This is Major Sheridan and his men," the loadmaster informed them.

Graham gulped slightly. Before him, waiting, were six heavily armed Royal Marines, all in green camouflage uniforms, their faces blackened with painted stripes. They looked tall, powerful, purposeful, and distinctly mean.

"Major," Graham said, extending his hand. "Thanks for bringing your lads out on short notice."

"Morning, boys," Barnwell tried, and the Marines gave him a slight but courteous nod.

"Not a problem," Sheridan told him. "Always glad to help. And it seems you've got yourself some dangerous people sailing around out there."

"I think we do," Graham agreed. "Have you been briefed on the plan?"

He had, of course. "We'll take one of our Zodiacs, but *Northumberland* will provide the major show of force. If anything goes wrong, the Lynx will hit the enemy vessel with gunfire or a guided missile if necessary."

"Crikey," Barnwell exclaimed again. "I don't think we need to—"

"The Navy likes to plan for *all* eventualities," Sheridan told him. "We'll embark on your authority, but the final go has to come from the Commander. He's on the line now," the major said. He handed Graham a cell phone and went to speak with his men.

"Paul, you old sea dog!" Graham said. "You've done me proud here. Can't thank you enough."

"Just so you know," Connolly said, "there's been a minor delay in informing the French Navy of this operation. But only a *minor* one."

"Roger that, Commander," Graham replied. "We'll be as quick as we can."

"Stay safe. And you must come by the house next time you decide to re-join civilization. Anita is dying to see you."

Graham signed off and put Connelly on speaker. "I'm

giving you the 'go' order, Major Sheridan," the commander said.

Sheridan nodded. "Right, lads." The six armed men stood up straight and carried out final inspections of each other's gear.

Graham clapped Barnwell on the shoulder. "Ready, Bazza?" his use of Barnwell's nickname an indication of the unusual situation they were in.

His reply was a grin, and they turned to follow the Marines as they jogged out to the windy deck and prepared to board their Zodiac.

Twenty minutes later, the world was a bumpy, confused whirl of sea spray and the most deafening engine noise Graham had ever suffered. Their Zodiac took advantage of the relatively calm waters, despite cool and occasionally blustery weather. It fizzed along the Channel's surface at over twenty knots. The Marines took this all in their stride, of course, but both Barnwell and Graham were left battling seasickness.

"Whose idea was this, again?" Barnwell complained, holding his turbulent stomach.

"You can thank me later," Graham replied, only narrowly hanging on to his breakfast himself. He turned back to see *HMS Northumberland*, dominant on the skyline, steaming steadily toward their target area while they swooped in at speed to surprise their prey.

"Lynx reports only one person on deck," Sheridan told Graham, yelling at almost full volume. "What do you think?"

Graham explained why he wasn't surprised. "Sounds

about right. Isn't that good news? I mean, only one adversary is better, right?"

Sheridan smiled thinly. "Depends on the decisions he makes, doesn't it?"

Nodding, Graham turned to Barnwell and found the constable staring resolutely at the gray flooring of the Zodiac, willing his rebellious gut to calm back down.

"Not far now, lad." In fact, Graham could make out the trawler in the far distance. It was coming closer at remarkable speed. "Look," he said. "What do you make of it?"

The boat had obviously been built at least fifty years before, and they were soon able to make out workaday patches on its blue hull. Barnwell looked crestfallen.

"It's not the same boat, sir."

"What? Are you sure?"

"The one I saw was red."

CHAPTER TWENTY-EIGHT

T HE DETECTIVE INSPECTOR bit his lip.
"Confirm just one individual in sight," a
marine reported, his binoculars glued to the
trawler. "No sign that he's seen us."

Graham found this hard to believe. The man on the
boat had a military helicopter flying overhead, a launch
containing six armed men barreling toward him at high-
speed, and a naval warship bringing up the rear. Graham
imagined that he was either paralyzed with fear or calling
someone for instructions. In any event, the Zodiac quickly
closed the distance, and Sheridan began calling over in pass-
able French.

A man appeared at the rail of the boat by the pilothouse,
but simply waved at the Zodiac before seeming to reach for
the throttle to gun the engines. He appeared to be preparing
to move out of the Zodiac's way. "I think we need to make
more of an impression," Sheridan told his men. "Firing
positions."

The six marines lined up, three kneeling in front, three
standing behind. They raised their assault rifles.

Barnwell cast a desperate glance at Graham. "Is this going to get out of hand, boss? I don't want to be on the news tonight for the wrong reasons, know what I mean?"

Graham nodded absentmindedly, but he was focused on the actions of the single man on board the other boat.

Sheridan was listening to his earpiece. "Roger, Henhouse." He roared to his men, "Heads down!"

They abandoned their firing positions and crouched down by the rail of the Zodiac. Graham heard a huge crescendo of sound, and instinctively ducked as the warship's Lynx came roaring over their heads, and directly above the French boat. It was so low they could feel the heat of the engine.

"Christ almighty!" Barnwell bellowed.

On the trawler, Hugo was battling sheer panic. Jean-Luc and Victor were both deep underwater, unaware of the drama that was occurring above their heads. After Jean-Luc had surfaced the previous day, he'd waited a scant twenty-four hours, the minimum safety margin, before returning to the wreck. Victor had gone with him, enlisted to assist with the flotation devices and additional air supplies. Faced with this show of force, Hugo, alone, cold, and terrified, had no plan beyond blustering his way out. He'd never figured on a party of soldiers showing up. As a shell landed in the water to his right with a whine and a splash, he saw that his options were vanishing. He threw up his hands in surrender and shut off the trawler's engine. Then he radioed down to the divers that they were about to be boarded. "I'm sorry, *mon ami*," he said. "Good luck."

"Royal Marines!" someone shouted behind him. "Don't move!" The six marines were on board before Hugo could blink twice. With them were two men. One looked a little familiar and was wearing a high-viz jacket with his name and rank emblazoned on the left breast. The other man was in an unadorned rain jacket.

"Do you speak English?" Graham asked him.

Hugo shrugged at first. "Yes, a little," he admitted, finally. "What is the problem today?"

"Stand down, marines! Fletcher, Norris, search the boat!" Sheridan ordered.

Barnwell took a long, hard look at Hugo before going with them, ducking to avoid the low ceiling as he descended into the interior.

"How long have you been out here?" Graham asked the Frenchman.

"A few days," Hugo responded, his voice shaking. His eyes darted between the Marines guarding him and Graham. "My colleagues are completing a dive as we speak." His tone was beseeching, as though begging Graham to believe him, but there was a touch of Parisian haughtiness in his tone.

"How many of you are there?"

"Three."

"And where were you headed?"

"We came from Cherbourg." There was a pause as Hugo considered how much he was willing to say. "We would have returned there eventually."

"No one else here, sir," Barnwell reported coming back on deck. The marines took up positions to guard the Frenchman and await the return of his two crewmen from the sea beneath. Barnwell was struck by the soldiers' quiet professionalism and their calm. They seemed to work in silence. They had said nary a word but seemed to work as one cohesive unit and know exactly what to do. He turned to look at Hugo and something clicked in his mind.

"Sir?" Barnwell said quietly in his boss' ear.

"Not now, lad."

"But I *have* seen this fella before, sir," Barnwell hissed in a rapid whisper. "Before the hurricane. You're right, this is the fishing boat that was in the wrong waters. Except it was red then, not blue."

"You sure?"

"Dead certain. It's definitely the same boat, and that's definitely the same guy."

Graham left Hugo with Barnwell and wandered around. He went below deck before returning to the Frenchman.

"Have you encountered either an Environmental Agency launch or a fishing boat named the *Cheeky Monkey*?"

Hugo shook his head resolutely. "I would have remembered."

"And the others?" he asked, pointing at the waves. "Might *they* be able to remember?"

Another shrug. "I can't speak for them."

"And when will they be able to speak for themselves, do you think?" Graham asked. "Is their dive likely to be a long one?"

Hugo checked his screens. "Victor will be coming up in a few minutes. Jean-Luc needs to stay down much longer, for decompression. It takes three or four hours, after a dive to these depths."

"Heroic," Graham noted. "And what have you found that's so important?"

Hugo bristled. "I'm not at liberty to say," he replied. He lifted his chin, "And I am not obliged to."

"So you weren't fishing, then?" Graham sought to confirm.

Hugo, bolder now, saw no reason to lie. "Does it look

like it?" He gestured around at his boat. There was absolutely no sign of any fishing equipment, or indeed any fish anywhere on it.

"What exactly are you doing out here, then?" Graham looked around him. This was no ordinary boat. Graham might not know much about the ways of the sea, but he understood that the instruments he'd seen below deck and in the pilothouse were most definitely out of the price range of the likes of Des Smith and his ilk.

Hugo sat. He folded his arms and almost comically, crossed his legs, clasping his hands around his knee. He pursed his lips. He looked out to sea and said nothing.

There was a strange, gassy sound from below and a cluster of objects enclosed in netting and buoyed by flotation devices rose from the deep to bob on the surface. "Victor is here," Hugo said simply.

"And Victor has brought something with him," Graham said. Then, quietly to Barnwell, "Here's where we find out whether I've made a massive fool of myself today."

Hugo deployed a small crane with a winch to grab the recovered objects and haul them up onto deck. He was clearly a novice, and kept sending the arm of the crane the wrong way, almost ditching the net and its contents into the sea. Finally, he set it down on the deck with a resounding *clunk*.

"Sounds important," Graham noted. "Maybe even valuable." Hugo detached the two inflatable buoys from the haul, allowing him access to the net-shrouded secret Victor had brought up from the depths.

At the rail of the ship, three marines were hauling the hapless diver onboard. He complained bitterly in French. The marines shepherded him to a quieter part of the boat where he took off his diving gear, and it was then that Barnwell decided to take a chance. He asked for a marine to give him a hand.

"What's this, Barry? You going swimming?" Graham asked, watching the marine dangling Barnwell precariously over the side of the boat.

The marine hauled the constable back up as he handed Graham a foot-long strip of the beaten-up hull that he'd torn off. "Have a look under the first layer of paint."

Graham took Victor's dive knife and scraped. Everything clicked. "Get Roach on the phone."

It took seconds. "How are you doing, sir?"

Graham ignored the question but fired back one of his own. "Greg Somerville's *Albatross*," he said. "Tell me about the collision."

Roach found the forensic report. "The boat has minor impact damage, some discoloration of the hull just under the..."

"*Which* color, lad?"

"Sorry, sir?"

"The discoloration. Which color?"

"Red, sir. Ferrari red. I saw it myself."

Graham glanced down at the strip of wood in his hands. The new blue paint gave way to a bright patch of its original color; a pleasingly brilliant red.

"Got 'em."

Barnwell was becoming impatient. "Is he communing with the fish down there or what?" he muttered to Graham.

"It's all about decompression," Graham explained. "If he comes up too quickly, he'll harm himself. Only way to do it safely is to go slow."

"Been diving before, have you, sir?" Barnwell asked.

"In Egypt," Graham said. "Long time ago. I also did a day of the police divers' course, just to get their perspective. Fascinating stuff and invaluable, but not a pleasant job, in my opinion."

Major Sheridan joined them. "Hello, sir. Everything all right?"

Graham nodded and shook the man's hand again. "Couldn't be better, under the circumstances. Your men and women have been excellent, major."

Sheridan reacted as though this were a routine response to his regiment's efforts, which it truly was. "Thought you should know that we'll be sailing south rather than taking the Lynx back. Someone felt that a robust display of Royal Navy strength off Gorey Harbor might be just what the doctor ordered."

"I think that's a great idea," Graham agreed. In truth, this had also been part of his initial request to Connolly, aimed at reassuring the fishermen who relished nothing more than demonstrations of British resolve at sea. "She'll be a sight for sore eyes, I'm sure."

"With these three men in your custody, think you'll be able to bring a successful case?" Sheridan asked.

"When we get back on land, we'll really test their mettle," Graham replied. "Then we'll see."

"Of course," Sheridan smiled. "The Commander told me that you were the best investigative mind in the Met."

"He embellishes," Graham said modestly.

"I think not," Sheridan replied with a grin.

Graham changed the subject. "Tell me, was that a live shell you dumped into the water earlier?"

An enigmatic smile played across Sheridan's lips. He merely paused as he peeled off to walk away, before saying

"All in a day's work, Detective Inspector, all in a day's work."

Graham regarded Victor and Hugo who were now sitting side by side on the boat's deck. Victor was spitting mad. He refused to speak in English, and swore colorfully at anyone who came close. He resembled an angry cat. Hugo was more composed.

"Barnwell, read them their rights. I'm going to see what all the fuss was about."

Just before Graham opened the net now laying bedraggled on the deck, he heard Hugo say, very quietly, "These are international waters. I am entitled."

"Entitled? To what?"

"To recover the treasure. To undertake reasonable means to retrieve it," Hugo told him.

Graham paid no attention to the trio of heavy, gold bars that were now exposed as he peeled away the nets. He looked up at Hugo. "And you think 'reasonable means' includes murder? Did you really end two lives to make sure no one else found this ancient gold?"

"*Non!*" Hugo replied. He looked horrified. And then, "Not me."

CHAPTER TWENTY-NINE

BARNWELL BREEZED IN through the double doors and strode over to Graham's open office door without stopping. "They bought the blue paint from Foley's. Arthur Foley confirms it, the day before the storm. All checks out. He was able to give me a copy of the receipt and everything."

"Excellent, Constable. This is more like it. We're building our case. Roach is over at the lab doing work on equipment we found on the boat."

"Have they said anything incriminating yet?"

"The two divers are not saying a word. I'm about to go interview the lead again, want to join me?"

"Erm, I think I'd rather stay out here in case Roachie calls in, if it's all the same to you, sir."

"Have it your way, Constable."

When he sat down, Graham surveyed the man across the table from him. Hugo was a slight, weedy-looking man, bespectacled and wide-eyed. He had dark circles under his eyes. His shoulders slumped, but he held Graham's gaze and offered him a weak smile.

"*Monsieur...*" Graham looked down at his notes, "Please confirm for the recording what you were doing out in the fishing lanes. You had been warned off at least once."

Hugo shook his head slowly, they had already been over this. "I would have thought it obvious by now, Inspector, that we were looking for treasure. Quite literally, gold. There have been rumors for decades about a shipwreck in these waters, a valuable one. I wanted to find it. I've been planning for years." He sat up straighter in his chair, and lifted his chin. "I would like to be released so that I can claim it. It is rightfully mine."

"Not so fast," Graham responded.

"Why not, Inspector? I haven't done anything wrong. Finders keepers, isn't that what you British say?"

"Did you ever see this man?" Graham pushed a photograph of Greg Somerville toward him.

Hugo looked at it carefully, fingering his glasses as he did so. "No."

"Not on your boat?"

"Not ever."

"*Monsieur*, this man's boat was in a collision with yours. We know this because traces of paint from your boat were found on its hull. Later, this man," Graham pointed at the photograph again, "turned up dead. Are you saying you know absolutely nothing about that?"

"*Alors*, no. I have never seen him. Are you suggesting we had something to do with his death?" Hugo's eyes were wide like those of a child's.

"I find it hard to believe that you wouldn't know that your boat collided with another."

Hugo shrugged. "If I were below deck..." The bookish man looked to the side. "When you are out at sea, Inspector, there are bumps and jolts all the time. It is nothing. I pay no attention."

"But you would have heard something."

Hugo suppressed a sigh but allowed a small smile to form on his lips. It felt good to talk to a man who knew less about being at sea than he did. "You don't understand, Inspector. What we were doing requires intense concentration. I am not paying attention to every rock and roll. And I wear headphones. "

"Hmm. I find it hard to believe you had no knowledge of what was happening above you. Your boat is hardly an ocean liner."

"Like I said, Detective Inspector, my attention was elsewhere."

"And you didn't see a body floating in the water? You know, *dead*?"

"*Non.*" Hugo pointed a soft white fingertip at the photograph in front of him. "I had nothing to do with his death, Inspector."

"You had something to do with it. Paint from your boat wouldn't be found on his if that weren't the case."

Hugo's expression was unreadable.

"All right then, where did you shore up when the hurricane hit? I assume you weren't out in that weather?" Graham asked.

"No, no, of course not. We came ashore and moored in a cove until the worst had passed. The hurricane was very frightening."

"What did you do?"

"Played cards, checked our equipment, slept. There was nothing we *could* do."

"So when did you paint the boat? It was red when my

officer saw you several days ago out in the fishing channels. Now it is blue."

Hugo shrugged. "Victor and Jean-Luc told me we needed to do repairs. Tidy her up, strengthen her hull. As you saw, she isn't in the greatest of shape. We took the opportunity of a few free hours before the storm arrived to paint her. Then we waited inside."

"Do you always do what your men tell you?"

"Yes."

Graham raised his eyebrows, inviting Hugo to say more.

"They are much more experienced than I. I would be a fool not to. My goal was to find the treasure. Everything else was secondary." Hugo pressed one finger on the bridge of his glasses frames and blinked.

"Secondary, eh?"

"Of course, I do not include death in that. Please do not assume from my words. I am very sorry for the man's passing, but I had nothing to do with it."

Graham sighed. He didn't feel like he was getting anywhere. "Very well. You will wait here. I'll be back to talk to you shortly." He stood and ended the interview for the recorder.

Outside the room, Barnwell came over to him. "Sir, Sergeant Roach's been on the phone. Dr. Tomlinson has a match for the murder weapon. Ballast weights. They match the victim's injuries."

"Yes! Can we link it to any of the men?"

"All evidence washed away, sir. They were using the weights to dive with."

"Damn."

"And, there's something else, sir. Dr. Tomlinson's now determined that the assailant was left-handed."

Graham's eyes lit up. "Constable, I could kiss you."

"I think I'd prefer that drink you promised, sir."

CHAPTER THIRTY

J EAN-LUC LOOKED warily at Graham as he came in the room. He had been sitting for over an hour and was becoming agitated. His heel bobbed up and down at a frenetic pace, turning his whole body into a wobbling mass of anxiety. He picked at the rough skin on his calloused hands.

Graham laid out two photographs. One was of the hull of the *Nautilus* where it had been painted over with blue paint, the other was of a streak of red on Greg Somerville's *Albatross*. Graham tapped the photograph of the *Nautilus'* hull. "Blue paint."

"*Oui.*"

"You painted the hull of your boat the day before the hurricane."

"*Oui,* we needed to do repairs."

"Under that blue paint we found red paint that matched that which was found on *this* boat." Graham tapped the photograph of the *Albatross*. "We can therefore prove a connection between your boat and this one, probably a collision of some kind."

Graham took out another photograph from the manila folder in front of him. This was of a webbed nylon belt. At intervals, metal weights were threaded onto it.

"Ballast weights," Jean-Luc said.

"Yes, what do you use them for?"

Jean-Luc shifted uncomfortably in his seat and eyed Graham from under a lock of his floppy hair. It hung over his eyes. "They help when we are descending in the water. All divers use them."

"We have found that the victim's injuries, the one whose boat had paint from your boat on it, can be shown to have been inflicted by these weights, your weights, the ones you dive with. He was killed with this weighted belt. Wouldn't have been hard, just a well-timed blow or two to the head." Graham leaned forward and looked at Jean-Luc intensely, both hands on the table. "What can you tell me about that?"

In response, Jean-Luc sat back in his chair, away from Graham, and rolled his head to one side. He looked down at the floor and then up at the ceiling. After a moment, he flicked the lock of hair out of his eye and regarded Graham. "He started it."

"Who did?"

"The other guy. He chased us, rammed us. He was mad. He jumped on board and started accusing us. We were sabotaging his research, damaging his equipment so he said. It was ridiculous, but he was angry. If we did damage his equipment, it was because of that fool, Hugo. He had no idea what he was doing half the time." Jean-Luc turned down the corners of his mouth, and spread his arms, palms upwards, as he raised his eyebrows, a typical Gallic shrug. "Maybe we ran over a buoy or two, it wasn't intentional."

"Go on."

"He wouldn't leave, he just kept shouting, and Victor got nervous. There was a fight between the guy and Victor, just some pushing and shoving, and he...he got hit with the weights."

"And then what happened?"

"He was dead. Poof. Victor dropped his body over the side."

"Just like that?"

Jean-Luc nodded. "Victor thought, with the hurricane coming in the next hours, his body would never be found and the boat would sink. I tried to stop him, to call you, the police, but he threatened me. He said he wasn't going to prison for the last years of his life and especially when we were close to crazy riches. He said we should put it out of our minds, that it was an accident, and that no one would know if we just kept our mouths shut." Jean-Luc regarded Graham's skeptical expression. "He'd already killed one man, Inspector. Being on a boat at sea with a murderer and a fool is not comfortable."

"So you're saying that Victor killed Mr. Somerville in a fight?"

"Yes."

"And then he threw his body overboard?"

"Yes."

"And you did not take part in his death or the disposal of his body?"

"No."

"Are you sure?" Graham held the man's gaze for long moment.

"Yes, of course I am sure." Jean-Luc didn't look away, but after a few seconds, there was a flicker in his eyes.

"But you didn't report the murder. And you carried on with your search even after you had come ashore."

"*Oui*, I am guilty of that." Jean-Luc looked down at the table. "And for that I am sorry."

"And *Monsieur* Fontenelle? What was his role in all this?"

"He had nothing to do with it. He was below deck. I doubt he knows anything at all. He isn't very bright about things at sea."

Graham ended the interview, and left, walking immediately into the room where Victor was being held.

The Frenchman was pacing the room. "Sit down." Victor stopped walking back and forth, but stood motionless. "I said, sit down," Graham growled. He glared, his cheeks flushing. Victor sat and leaned forward on his forearms, meeting Graham's glare with one of his own.

"Your friend, Jean-Luc, denies killing Mr. Somerville." Graham showed Somerville's photograph to Victor.

"I do not know him."

"He was killed on your boat."

Victor frowned. "I have never seen him before."

"Jean-Luc is blaming you for the killing."

Victor shrugged and scratched his grey stubble. "I am not lying. This is the truth. If someone on our boat killed him, it must have been Jean-Luc, not me." He sat back in his chair and folded his arms.

"What's the status, sir?"

"Jean-Luc Bisson and Victor Delormé are both blaming the other like the mercenary rats that they are. Jean-Luc has implicated himself in the cover-up, but he maintains Somerville was the aggressor and claims it was Victor who killed him. Victor, on the other hand, denies any knowledge of Somerville's death, or even Somerville himself, but if he was killed then it must have been Jean-Luc who did it according to him. Fontenelle, meanwhile, is claiming that he heard and saw nothing of Somerville, dead or alive." Graham tossed his pen on his desk. "What a mess."

"There's no honor among thieves, sir."

"So what have we got, Barnwell?" Graham sat back in his chair. He had a cup of steaming hot jasmine tea on his desk. "We can connect the two boats. We can prove our victim was killed with the weights. But we can't prove which one of them did it."

"Is there any evidence to connect them to the missing Mr. Crouch?"

Graham scratched his head. "Nope."

"Perhaps we were wrong. Maybe that case isn't connected at all. The evidence isn't leading us in that direction so perhaps we need to put 'informed inference' to one side this time."

Graham looked at Barnwell carefully. He leaned back even further in his chair and rubbed his eyebrows with the heels of his hands, screwing his eyes up tight as he let out a long exhale. "Yes, you're right, Barnwell. I think we've reached the end of the line with using inference to inform the direction this case is heading. Only hard evidence matters at this point."

There was silence as they both pondered what the evidence told them. There was no getting around the fact that they couldn't prove beyond a doubt who had killed Greg Somerville. Barnwell's face suddenly brightened. "What about the assailant being left-handed, sir. Why don't we set them a test?"

Graham's eyes slowly widened. "Brilliant, Barnwell!"

An hour later, Barnwell brought the men's statements

into Graham. He'd typed them up, and together they watched as one by one, the three men read his over and signed it.

All of them gripped the pen with their right hand.

"Damn," Graham said outside the room where Hugo had just added a signature to his statement that claimed no knowledge of Greg Somerville or his death.

Barnwell looked at the DI warily. Graham was tapping the statement with his pen before he came to a sudden decision. "We need more. How many hours do we have left before we have to charge them?"

Barnwell looked at his watch. "Five, sir."

"Get Roach on the phone, get him to go over the victim's belongings, including his boat, again. We need to connect Victor or Jean-Luc to our victim. I'll interview them again and again, if necessary. One of them might break down. Unless we get a confession or more hard evidence, the CPS won't uphold a charge of murder."

"And the leader of the expedition? Mr. Fontenelle?"

"He seems completely out of his depth, if you'll excuse the pun. I think we can get him on a host of maritime infractions," Graham said. "But I think he's in the clear for the murder.

"Are you sure, sir?"

"Yes, yes, Barnwell. Come on, chop, chop. Get Roach on the blower. We don't have much time."

Inside the interview room, Hugo was very still. He couldn't help but overhear what was being said by the two police officers. As he sat, silent and alone, no one saw the smirk that dared his lips to curl before, like a genie in a puff of smoke, it vanished.

CHAPTER THIRTY-ONE

T HE MICROWAVE IN the break room pinged for the third time and Barnwell opened the door. He balanced the carton on his fingertips, quickly pulled it out, and tipped the contents onto a paper plate before the scorching heat burned his fingers. Next to it were two more plates similarly laden.

"Mmmm, microwave lasagna. Just what I want for my dinner when I get home," Janice said, sarcastically, bringing in two mugs and setting them in the sink.

"You'll be glad to hear, then, that this isn't for you. In accordance with Home Office regulations, it's time for our prisoner's lunch. This is what's on today's menu; the best microwave lasagna and peas our local police café can offer," Barnwell said, as he placed each plate of food on a plastic tray and added a single paper cup of water and a spoon.

"I hope they appreciate you," Janice said as she ran the tap to wash the mugs. "It's more than I suspect they deserve."

"Well, lucky for them, if we don't turn something up in

the next hour, they won't have to appreciate me for much longer."

"No progress?"

"Nah, Roachie says that they can't find anything to connect the victim to either of the two men. We have to let them go or charge them with lesser offenses at two o'clock."

"What about the other guy?"

"The DI has eliminated him." Barnwell leaned back against the counter wiping his hands on a dishtowel. "I think he's being a bit premature, to be honest. I mean, who's to say? The DI seems to think he doesn't have it in him, but that's not evidence is it? And doesn't he tell us to follow where the evidence leads? We don't *have* any evidence, therefore we shouldn't be making judgments one way or another."

"Careful, Bazza, they'll be court-martialing you for insubordination if you're not careful. Or perhaps charging you with thinking too much," Harding said, taking the towel from him and wiping her own hands on it before slapping it back onto his chest with a smile.

Barnwell picked up one of the trays. "Just doesn't seem right to me. But I'm only a lowly constable, what do I know?"

"Grub's up," he announced as he opened the door to Jean-Luc's cell. The Frenchman was sitting on the cell bench with his eyes closed. He stirred and twisted around as Barnwell handed him his food tray and immediately tucked in, taking large, fast mouthfuls.

Victor, however, made no such move when Barnwell opened the door of his cell. Faced with a wall of indifference, Barnwell left the tray on the floor by the door. He checked his watch. "You've got ten minutes, then I take the food away."

Finally, it was Hugo's turn. They were out of cells, and he was still in the interview room. Hugo wrinkled his nose at the sight of the food placed in front of him and looked up at Barnwell.

"Like it or lump it, mate. That's all you're getting."

Hugo sighed and fingered the spoon. "A napkin, Constable?"

"What?"

"A napkin, could I have a napkin?" He gave Barnwell a facetious smile. "Please."

Barnwell muttered something inaudible and left. He went back into the break room and ripped a sheet from the roll of paper towels that stood on the counter. Silently, he returned to the interview room and dangled it in front of Hugo's face. Hugo, who was nibbling at his lasagna, took it from him and dabbed at his lips.

After locking him in, Barnwell stood at the door, tapping his palm with the key. He went back into the break room and ripped off two more sheets of paper towel. He opened up Jean-Luc's cell once more. "Here," he said handing him the sheet.

At Victor's cell door, Barnwell slid open the shutter and peeked inside. He got out his keys again and opened the door. "Changed your mind, eh?"

Victor had picked up his tray and, balancing it on his knees, was chewing slowly and methodically. He ignored the paper towel Barnwell proffered. The constable left it on the seat beside him. Outside, Barnwell allowed this heavy bunch of keys to retract slowly on their key chain as he looked down the hallway to their open plan office at the end. He walked the few steps to DI Graham's office.

"Sir?"

"Yes, Barnwell? What is it?"

"I think I know who did it, sir." Barnwell's body was tense, the expression on his face serious, his forefinger pointed to emphasize the point he was about to make. "It was just now, when I was taking them their food. The killer, I think he's am...ambi... Ugh, what's that word where they use both hands to do things? My brother's like it. Kicks a ball with his left foot, holds a bat in his right hand."

"Do you mean ambidextrous, Constable?"

"That's it, ambi...thingy. Well, I've just seen him eating," Barnwell's eyes darted around the room, replaying the scene in his mind. "You know, with his left hand. The leader guy. It was that Hugo who killed Greg Somerville."

Graham sat at his desk, twirling his pen in his fingers. A cup of tea sat cooling in front of him, unusually forgotten such was the depth of his reverie. He was engaging in a spate of deep reflection into his personal prejudices. Barnwell's revelation about Hugo had caused him to examine them closely and not without some shame.

There was a knock at his office door. Roach peeked his head in.

"Sir?'

"Yes, Roach."

The sergeant sheepishly held up a plastic bag. Inside it was a piece of paper.

Graham glared at his sergeant and stood to walk over to take the bag from him. He read the lines of print that was written on the paper inside it. "Where did you get this?"

"It was tucked away in this backpack, sir." Roach held the straps of a battered navy blue pack between his gloved fingertips. "It was left in a locker in the Harbormaster's building. He found it during his weekly cleanup."

Graham let out a big sigh and handed back the bag with Matt Crouch's suicide note in it. "Poor guy. Imagine finding out that your wife was having an affair with your best mate *and* that the baby she's carrying isn't yours. What is it with some humans that they seem bound and determined to annihilate one another?" He shook his head, not for the first time achingly depressed by the potential for cruelty exhibited by a portion of the population.

"And it says here, that the best mate and the wife admitted it to him. D'you think they did that when he came back off Des Smith's boat that morning? So they were lying to Janice when she interviewed them? She said the friend's face was bruised like he'd been in a fight."

"I shouldn't wonder."

"What should I do, sir?"

"Record the evidence. Then go and arrest Crouch's wife and her boyfriend. Take Janice with you. Interview them and use all that knowledge you gained studying for your Sergeants' exam to come up with as many charges as you can think of. I can name at least two. One starts with "wasting" and ends in "time," the other, "perverting" and "justice." While you're doing that, I'll finish up here. At least now I can stop trying to turn myself into a modern-day Houdini trying to solve a crime that doesn't exist."

Graham went outside into the reception area. "Barnwell! Come with me. No 'ifs or buts,' this time. You're about to attend your first murder investigation interview."

"It wasn't Hugo," Jean-Luc was adamant.

"We have him banged to rights, which means there's no doubt he was the murderer. We have evidence to prove it, and we know you are lying," Graham said. "You might as well tell the truth."

Jean-Luc stood, his teeth bared. His entire body was taut, the whites of his eyes stood out against the black of his pupils. Barnwell watched anxiously and shifted the weight of his body forward on his chair. Graham regarded the Frenchman mildly.

Jean-Luc turned away and took three paces, clenching his fists before tipping his head back, his mouth wide open as he laid bare the frustration, anger, and bitterness that roared from him in a deafening howl.

There was a hurried knock on the door. Roach appeared. "Everything all right, sir?" he asked looking around the room.

"Yes, thank you Roach. Everything is just fine."

Jean-Luc threw himself on the chair and put his head face-down on the table, his arms dangling between his wide spread legs.

"So tell me what happened, Jean-Luc."

There was a mumble from under the table.

"Sit up, and tell me for the recorder, please."

Like a truculent teen, Jean-Luc straightened and began to tell the story, slowly at first. "Hugo rammed the scientist's boat. Only Hugo could be useless enough to hit another lone boat in the middle of a huge stretch of water." Jean-Luc tapped his thumbs against the flat surface of the table. "The guy in the other boat was mad as hell. I was telling the truth when I said he accused us of damaging his equipment. Victor argued with him, and there was a fight, but it was Hugo who hit him with the weights. He died instantly. It was crazy."

Graham imagined all three men yelling in French, gesticulating wildly at one another on a boat in the midst of the English Channel.

"Why didn't you report the death?"

"Hugo didn't want to stop our search. He had planned it for years, made sacrifices, he said. We had all worked so hard and the prize was so great." Jean-Luc looked up at the ceiling and screwed his eyes tight shut. "We tipped his body overboard and left his boat for the storm to deal with. Then we came ashore and painted the *Nautilus*. Over the hours of the storm we discussed what to do if his body washed up. Hugo told us that if we found the shipwreck, as the financier of the expedition only he could claim the bounty. It was a threat. He said if we were questioned, we should keep him out of it, and he would make it worth our while later. Me and Victor decided that we would deny all knowledge of the scientist, and if forced to, take the blame ourselves. We figured we'd go back to Hugo for the money later, when it was all over."

"But that's not what you did, is it? You blamed each other."

Jean-Luc stared at Graham, blinking. "*Bien sûr*. Of course. Victor would never confess, I knew that. It's dog eat dog on the high seas, Inspector."

CHAPTER THIRTY-TWO

"NOT SURE HOW to put this, sir. I think we've got a lead on Mrs. Taylor's recent 'visitations,'" Roach said at Graham's office doorway.

It was mid-morning, and the Gorey police officers were all relaxing, appreciative of the lull in police activity now that their cells were empty. The three Frenchmen had been arraigned in court that morning and were now on their way to Jersey's HM Prison La Moye.

At the sound of Sergeant Roach's words, Graham was up and marching into the reception area in a second. There he found an unkempt little man, older than himself, looking distinctly uncomfortable. "This is Ernie Prescott. Ernie, why don't you tell the Detective Inspector what you told me?" Roach said.

The man spoke in a soft, uncertain mutter that took some deciphering. "Well, you see," he began, "I was down the pub a few weeks ago. I'd had a few, you know. And this fella, a guy I've known for years, says he's got something special that I might want to buy."

Graham nodded, desperately hoping that yet more of

his precious time wasn't about to be frittered away on nonsense.

"Plenty of dodgy stuff gets bought and sold in pub car parks, sir," Roach reminded the DI.

"I do know that, Sergeant." Then, Graham asked, "What was it that was 'special?'"

"Well, I'm something of an amateur naturalist," Ernie Prescott told him.

Roach blushed. "I don't think we need to know about your personal habits, thank you very much. Could you just stick to describing the item you bought?"

Graham held back a huge gust of mirth by the narrowest margin. "You're thinking of a 'naturist', Sergeant."

"Oh." Roach blushed again.

Graham nodded at the man in front of them. "This man has an enthusiasm for the natural world. You know, David Attenborough, and what-have-you."

"Roger that," Roach said sheepishly.

"Quite so, quite so," the little man was saying. "And my friend from the pub offered me something I couldn't refuse."

The voice came as a surprise. "A golden tamarin." Sergeant Harding strode in, carrying several eight by five-inch photographs. "Rare, beautiful, exceptionally expensive, and quite difficult to keep," she told them all. "Very nimble little blighters, too. Few cages can keep them for long." She waved the prints she held in her hand.

The little man sighed.

Harding laid the photographs out on a table. "Those camera phone images Mrs. Taylor gave us were next to useless," she said. "So I installed a suite of infra-red cameras. Borrowed them from Special Branch," she told Graham.

"Very resourceful, Sergeant."

Janice continued, "They're movement-activated, so each time the monkey—"

"Tamarin," the little man corrected. "His name's Harvey."

"*Who cares?*" mouthed Roach to Janice over the man's head.

"Each time the *tamarin* went rampaging through Mrs. Taylor's kitchen the camera went off." The pictures were wonderfully clear. They showed the tiny creature galloping up the side of a stack of metal shelves, and then delightedly throwing, pushing to the ground, and nibbling everything he found up there.

"The little blighter!" Graham exclaimed. Then he turned to Ernie Prescott and said gravely, "Selling and owning such a creature is a criminal offense."

"Aye," the man admitted. "That'd be right." His shoulders slumped. "And I wouldn't be here now but for that blogger who wrote all about the goings-on at the White House Inn. Once I realized Harvey had gone, I had no idea where he might be. But when I read about what was happening at the Inn, well, I recognized the behavior, you see. I put two and two together. Then, when I went down there to get him, the bloody woman who owns the hotel called you lot!" he ended indignantly.

Roach found the blog entry in Solomon's *Gorey Gossip*. "Makes a bit more sense than a ghost, doesn't it?"

"Mrs. Taylor had a *fit* when she found out it was an animal causing chaos in her kitchen. I got the keepers from the monkey compound at Jersey Zoo round there sharpish, and they tracked it down to a covered pipe space in the corner of the kitchen, but she was virtually hysterical," Harding said.

"Can't say I blame her, but I'm mostly relieved that another of Gorey's seemingly inexplicable mysteries has been resolved and even more relieved that Mrs. Taylor will now stop badgering us about it. I'll go and see her in the next few days," Graham promised. "Whatever I think about her…beliefs, she's certainly been through it, poor woman. Will the zoo keep the monkey?"

"Yes, sir," Janice said.

Graham turned to Prescott. "Sergeant Roach," he said, "would you favor charging this man, under the circumstances?"

Roach thought for a second. "I'd give him a stern warning, sir, with a commitment that he will not keep any exotic pets henceforth. And I'd invite the health inspectors to visit his home."

Graham escorted the man to the door. "Stay out of trouble, Ernie. And definitely stay out of pub car parks at night, all right?"

The little man left and scuttled home.

"Aaaaand another one bites the dust," Harding observed. "We're getting good at this, aren't we?"

EPILOGUE (PART ONE)

The Gorey Gossip
Wednesday, November 21st

Isn't it amazing the things that can change in a single week?

As I write, three Frenchmen are sitting in jail cells, detained courtesy of Gorey Constabulary, awaiting their fate on charges including murder, accessory to murder, piracy, and criminal trespassing. This reporter has learned that the three men, inspired by tales of sunken treasure, were diving on an uncharted wreck within the Thames sea area, not twenty miles from where you now sit. We have only initial findings, but my background in historical research has enabled me to fill in the blanks.

It was 13th March, 1587 — a Friday, of course. A fleet of three carracks — a very old style of sailing ship that gave rise to the more famous galleon — were transiting the English Channel on their way to Holland from the New World. All three were owned and operated by Portuguese traders who had made several risky journeys across the Atlantic, returning crates of the choicest valuables to a well-connected merchant based at the port city of Rotterdam. He paid them top dollar, and this led to them taking risks.

We don't know if the storm hit quickly, or if the mariners chose to risk what they knew would be a difficult transit. But one of the ships, the *Pretty Lady*, found herself in trouble and sank in the storm. We can only imagine that she was lost with all hands.

After that, there were just rumors. No one knew exactly where the ship had sunk, and the passage of time dimmed memories and the regrettably piecemeal historical record. But from my research, I've been able to establish that the wreck discovered last week was the carrack that went missing on that fateful Friday, well over four hundred years ago. The *Pretty Lady* must be one of the most exciting finds in the history of marine archaeology, and to be at the center of such a discovery is a tremendous thrill.

But now, the lawyers will descend. Ownership of the wreck is naturally contested between the descendants of the Dutch traders who commissioned the journey, the families of the Portuguese mariners, and the indigenous people of South America, whose gold and timber was so ruthlessly exploited. If they are found guilty, those who discovered the wreck will be forced to forfeit their rights to the treasure because of their criminal actions. No quick solution can be expected, and my sources have warned of a very protracted legal battle that could take many years.

In the meantime, we grieve for our recent losses, and we pray for the families forever changed by connection to this tragic story. Yet again, greed and selfishness made a bid to triumph over truth and justice but were found wanting. It has been a privilege to help reveal this case to the good people of Gorey and to the world, and I owe this wonderful community my heartfelt thanks for their warmth, and especially for their timely and accurate information. Remember, if you see something…'Say it to Solomon.'

EPILOGUE (PART TWO)

HUGO FONTENELLE CONTINUED to maintain his innocence but was found guilty of the murder of Greg Somerville and jailed for twenty years. It was recommended that he serve at least twelve before being eligible for parole. Jean-Luc Bisson and Victor Delormé were tried for conspiracy and accessory to murder and asked the judge to take into consideration eight other counts relating to maritime offenses. They were jailed for ten years.

At their trials, both divers maintained they had no idea that Fontenelle was as callous and calculating as he proved to be. Had they known, they both claim they would not have embarked on the expedition to recover the lost treasure with him.

Cheryl Crouch confirmed that on the morning of her husband's disappearance, he had confronted her with rumors that she and Phil Whitmore were having an affair.

At that time, she admitted the relationship, and there was an altercation between the two men. She and Whitmore were charged with obstruction and were ordered to undertake 100 hours community service each. Once complete, they moved to Whitmore's native Yorkshire where they lived quietly in the countryside until their eventual breakup five years later after a paternity test showed that Mr. Whitmore was not the father of the daughter born to Mrs. Crouch following her husband's death.

The coroner recorded a verdict of death by suicide in the case of the disappearance of Matt Crouch. His body was never found. It is believed that he threw himself overboard and drowned in despair over the revelation of his wife's affair with Phil Whitmore. A small but vocal group continue to suggest that Crouch faked his own death, and at least one person claims to have seen him on a beach in the South of France. Sightings of him around Gorey persist, especially following bad weather. The story of his disappearance has since passed into Gorey folklore joining those of the "Beast of Jersey" and "Marjorie's Monkey."

Kevin Cummings resigned his post as the regional director of the local SeaWatch chapter and was last heard from scaling Sydney Harbor Bridge to protest the sailing of the oil-company-owned ship, *Broadlands*, which was traveling to join an oil drilling fleet in Antarctica. Tamsin Porter returned to the mainland and now teaches a marine biology course at the University of Portsmouth.

Des Smith continues to roam the high seas and never fails to miss an opportunity to regale any audience with his views, regardless of their interest in them. He did not follow through with his threat to blockade a major French harbor on account of DI Graham pointing out that the Frenchmen arrested for Somerville's murder were not fishermen. Quotas have not been raised, suspicion between the fishing fraternity and the government is still deep, and the French fishermen continue to disembark on Jersey and rile up the locals. In fact, nothing appears to have changed since the "Fishermen Frenzy" protests.

Following an incident where he insulted the Lord Lieutenant of Jersey, a representative of the Queen and the *de facto* head of state for the island, Jersey Coastguard Commander, Brian Ecclestone was removed from his post and promptly reassigned to an even quieter Coastguard station in Wales. Two of his new staff resigned almost immediately.

Freddie Solomon's talent for writing salacious, sensational, and popular articles about the events of Gorey continues unabated and is matched only by his ability to earn the Detective Inspector's enduring contempt.

Sergeant Janice Harding has become fast friends with Mrs. Taylor and can often be seen at the White House Inn, exchanging gossip and 'flying the flag,' as the sergeant likes to put it. She's carefully thinking about moving in with Jack Wentworth but is hesitant to tell her grandmother.

Sergeant Jim Roach's forensic career continues apace, and he will now spend two days a week on the mainland to study with Dr. Miranda Weiss, Adjunct Professor in criminology at the University of Southampton and Head of Forensics for the Jersey Police. He will also continue to work with Dr. Tomlinson in Gorey and St. Helier. He claims to never have been happier in his life.

Constable Barry Barnwell began a brief lecture tour, retelling the stories of his maritime exploits at schools and youth clubs. He recently requested a month's special leave in order to climb a challenging Alpine peak. He continues to hone his ability for critical and independent thinking, has developed a new passion for self-help books, recently limited his consumption of the *Daily Mail* newspaper to once a week on Saturdays, and has sworn off reading the *Gorey Gossip* entirely.

Laura Beecham and Detective Inspector David Graham can frequently be seen together, either strolling around town or at the Bangkok Palace. David recently received a

"Gold Star for Bravery" for his daring forays into the spicier corners of the Palace's menu awarded by the stunned (and frequently very concerned) Bangkok Palace staff. Graham continues to be "excessively busy," but the couple does find enough time to be together amid the daily challenges of their respective work schedules and Graham recently booked himself some much-needed vacation time, surprising Laura with tickets for a week-long cruise in the Caribbean.

To get your free copy of *The Case of the Screaming Beauty,* the prequel to the Inspector David Graham series, plus two more books, updates about new releases, exclusive promotions, and other insider information, sign up for Alison's mailing list at:

https://www.alisongolden.com/graham

BOOKS BY ALISON GOLDEN

FEATURING REVEREND ANNABELLE DIXON

Death at the Café (Prequel)

Murder at the Mansion

Body in the Woods

Grave in the Garage

Horror in the Highlands

Killer at the Cult

FEATURING DIANA HUNTER

Hunted (Prequel)

Snatched

Stolen

Chopped

Exposed

ABOUT THE AUTHOR

Alison Golden is the *USA Today* bestselling author of the Inspector David Graham mysteries and Reverend Annabelle Dixon cozy mysteries. As A.J. Golden, she writes the Diana Hunter thriller series.

Alison was raised in Bedfordshire, England. Her aim is to write stories that are designed to entertain, amuse, and calm. Her approach is to combine creative ideas with excellent writing and edit, edit, edit.

Alison is based in the San Francisco Bay Area with her husband and twin sons. She splits her time between London and San Francisco.

For up-to-date promotions and release dates of upcoming books, sign up for the latest news here: https://www.alisongolden.com/graham.

For more information:
www.alisongolden.com
alison@alisongolden.com

facebook.com/alisongolden.books

twitter.com/alisonjgolden

instagram.com/alisonjgolden

THANK YOU

Thank you for taking the time to read *The Case of the Pretty Lady*. If you enjoyed it, please consider telling your friends or posting a short review. Word of mouth is an author's best friend and very much appreciated.

Thank you,

Made in the USA
Middletown, DE
09 July 2020